The Gun Runners

The Civil War over, Captain Sam Curtis just wants to return home, but instead finds himself embroiled in a covert operation to smuggle weapons to Mexican rebels, fighting to rid themselves of Emperor Maximilian I and the French forces who have invaded their country.

Betrayed and left for dead by the ex-Confederate, Henry Fontaine, he faces many obstacles in his quest to recover the weapons and complete his mission. Aided by Sergeant Ben Boyd and the fiery Consuela Martinez, he battles bandits, the French Army and royalist guerrillas, commanded by the ruthless Colonel Dupin, before facing his enemies in a final showdown at the rebel held town of Tacambaro.

By the same author

The Devil's Payroll

The Gun Runners

Paul Green

A Black Horse Western

ROBERT HALE · LONDON

ISBN 978-0-7090-9766-2

Robert Hale Limited
Clerkenwell House
Clerkenwell Green
London EC1R 0HT

www.halebooks.com

Typeset by
Derek Doyle & Associates, Shaw Heath
Printed and bound in Great Britain by
CPI Antony Rowe, Chippenham and Eastbourne

Dedicated to the memory of my uncle,
Eamer Coughlan, a fine teller of stories

CHAPTER ONE

Captain Sam Curtis mopped the sweat from his dust-caked features with a worn bandanna and then knotted it back in place around his neck. It was over a month since General Lee had surrendered at Appomatox but the war was not quite over yet for Sam and the six men trailing through the Chihuahuan desert behind him. Shading his eyes from the sun's glare, he looked up to the canyon a few miles ahead and beyond it to the shimmering peaks of the Pecos Mountains. His horse slowed beneath him as he raised a telescope to his right eye and Sergeant Ben Boyd drew alongside.

'Do you see anything, sir?'

'No sign of them. Go on, you take a look.'

Boyd took the instrument from him and quickly scanned the horizon but then sighed and shook his head. Sam looked into the sergeant's one piercing blue eye. A black patch covered the empty socket where the left one had been before a bullet tore it out at Galveston. Boyd held his gaze and shrugged resignedly, both men reflecting on the apparent futility of their mission.

'I guess Fontaine and his men could be anywhere but that canyon's a good place to hide. Do you think it's worth a try, Sergeant?'

'Yes, sir. There's no place else round here they're likely to be, anyhow.'

Sam nodded and urged his weary mount forward. General Sheridan's orders had been very specific. Colonel Henry Lucius Fontaine and the rag tag remains of his regiment now numbered five or six men at most, following desertions and those who had reluctantly agreed to surrender. They were the last of the diehards and were to be brought back alive to what remained of the military post at El Paso, which was currently undergoing reconstruction. Sheridan had been explicit in his instructions that the men be taken prisoner if at all possible, a condition that applied most especially to Fontaine. Sam could only presume that the general intended to have them put on trial and hanged for murder since, legally, their insistence on continuing to fight and kill Union soldiers following the surrender was just that.

As they drew nearer, Sam realized that the climb was far too steep for the horses. He halted at the foot of the canyon and gave the order to dismount, then summoned Ralph Paterson, a lanky, red-haired youth whom he knew to be good with horses.

'You stay here and look after our mounts. Give

them each a rub down and some water while we're gone.'

The trooper saluted smartly and got to work right away while Sam started his ascent, the others falling in behind him. He heard Baker and Macdonald muttering to each other and smiled as Sergeant Boyd gruffly ordered them to keep quiet, anticipating his own command. If Fontaine and his men really were in the canyon, the last thing he wanted was to alert them. The path was narrow but steep and uneven so their progress was slow. Then it wound around a bend past a massive boulder and they were no longer able to see Paterson's tiny figure below. They reached a small plateau and Sam signalled for them to take a rest since there was no point in finding the enemy if they were too exhausted to fight.

After they had been sitting for a few minutes, Sam glanced at his pocket watch. It was just past noon and getting hotter. Arne Svenson was sitting next to him and he sensed the farmhand from Iowa suddenly tense his broad shoulders. Svenson's famously acute hearing was rumoured to be the result of straining to work out what his Swedish parents were saying in their heavily accented American. Whatever the reason, it was an admired quality which had saved lives on more than one occasion. After a moment, he pointed upwards and then Sam heard a muffled voice say something about 'giving up' before it was contradicted by another, slightly louder voice. Boyd nodded to show that he had heard it too and the signal was passed along so that each man knew there were people above them.

Sam gestured toward Zeke Winters, a stocky, dark-haired trooper who was the shortest member of the group, and pointed ahead. Winters nodded and went on in front of them. Being smaller than average, he was more likely to be able to spot the enemy without being seen. Winters was agile and slunk, cat-like below the wall of rock to their left. As he rounded another bend the path climbed higher and ended in a ledge, above which there was a larger plateau. Sam saw him peep over it and then gesture for them all to get down lower and stay quiet. Winters crept back towards them and held up five fingers to indicate the number of men he had seen. Further gestures told Sam that all were armed and one was on lookout, armed with a rifle.

Boyd handed Winters a short knife and then looked at Sam, who nodded his agreement. Killing the lookout might enable them to surprise his compan-ions and take them prisoner without a shot being fired. Each man drew his revolver as Winters crept up to the ledge once more. He paused and then suddenly sprang, thrusting his blade into the lookout's ribs when the man turned away briefly, muffling his victim's cries with his other hand. The others had all reached the edge of the plateau before the dead man hit the ground, Sam in the lead, and found themselves behind four dishevelled looking men in tattered grey uniforms sitting around a makeshift camp.

One of the men stood up and turned to see them. It was clearly Fontaine as he wore a colonel's insignia and his uniform, though worn, was in better condition than that of his men. His right hand hovered near his holster but he did not go for it, having coolly appraised the odds against a successful outcome.

'You'd better tell your men to hand over their weapons,' Sam told him.

The others turned then and two reluctantly raised their hands. A third went for his gun and Sam fired, the bullet hitting him neatly between the eyes but Fontaine did not move.

'I won't ask again,' warned Sam.

'Do as he says, men. Take off your gun-belts.' The words were uttered calmly, in a southern drawl, and Fontaine did not take his cold grey eyes off Sam as he spoke.

'You too, Fontaine, and that fancy sword as well.'

The colonel reluctantly removed his weapons and tossed them on to the ground in front of him. Svenson was then ordered to search the three men for any hidden guns.

'I believe it is customary, even among uncivilized Yankees, to salute a senior officer,' remarked Fontaine.

'The war's over. You ain't a colonel no more,' said Boyd.

'That's right,' added Sam. 'You continued to fight after a peace was concluded, which means you and your men have committed treason and we're not in the habit of saluting criminals, whether in or out of uniform.'

Fontaine shot him a look of contempt. 'The terms of surrender imposed on my countrymen were such that no man of honour can regard himself bound by them. It pains me to give up my sword on such terms, Captain.'

'Well, painful or not, you don't have any choice. I'm Captain Curtis and this is Sergeant Boyd. We've orders to take you to the military post at El Paso.'

Fontaine stroked his trim red whiskers thoughtfully. 'As you are doubtless aware, I am Colonel Fontaine.' He gestured to a heavyset individual with a straggly beard and dark, almost black eyes. 'This is Corporal Milton and over there is Private Gates.' Gates had a faintly simian appearance and wisps of straw-like fair hair showed beneath his cap. Both men saluted smartly as they were introduced, presumably wishing to set an example to their 'uncivilized' captors.

'Do you have any horses, Captain?' asked Fontaine hopefully.

'Our horses are down below,' said Sam. 'I'm afraid you three will have a long walk to El Paso. Now, once you've buried your dead, we'll get going.'

The two dead confederates were buried under heaps of stones and Fontaine then read the Twenty-Third Psalm over them while the others stood with their heads bowed. The prisoners went in front, their hands bound, and were watched carefully by Boyd.

As they rounded the bend by the large boulder they had passed during their ascent, Sam looked down and saw with alarm that the horses had disappeared. Peering over, he thought he saw someone lying on the ground but could not be certain.

'Stop for a moment,' he told the others as he fumbled for his telescope, then he realized with dismay that he had left it in his saddle-bag.

'Is something wrong, sir?' Boyd asked without turning round.

'I can't see the horses or any sign of Paterson.'

'Perhaps he took 'em into some shade somewhere. There were a couple of caves down there as I recall.'

'Yes, that must be it,' Sam agreed reluctantly, not wanting to worry the men.

When they reached the bottom, however, there was indeed no sign of the horses but only what was left of Paterson. The sight of his gouged out eye sockets, the opening in his stomach where the entrails had been removed and the stench of burnt flesh were too much even for a hardened veteran like Boyd. He turned away gasping while Sam himself was violently sick.

'Damned Apaches,' muttered Milton. 'I'd sure like to get my hands on 'em.'

'Be careful what you wish for, Corporal. There's likely to be more of them than there are of us,' remarked Fontaine drily.

Suddenly Macdonald pointed into the distance. 'Look, there's two of 'em chasin' some woman.'

13

'Give me that rifle,' commanded Sam, and Svenson passed it to him. As he took aim he saw that the woman's horse had just been shot from under her by one of the Apaches in pursuit. She rolled over in the sand, stumbled to her feet and started to run in desperation. She screamed as her hair was seized from behind. Sam squeezed the trigger. The Apache tumbled backwards from his horse and his companion hesitated in his pursuit, giving the girl time to get away. Sam fired again and hit the other Apache in the shoulder. He swayed in the saddle and made to ride off. Sam's third shot hit the horse, which rolled over and the rider was crushed underneath it as they fell together, his injury having prevented him from being able to jump clear.

The girl was now stumbling across the sand towards them and Sam went to meet her. She fell sobbing against him as they came together and he spoke soothingly to reassure her that she was now safe. She drank greedily from the canteen he handed her and then slowly started to recover. She wore what had once been a very pretty but was now a quite soiled and torn blue dress. Her raven hair was in disarray and her face streaked with grime and dried blood. Yet even in her current state, it was clear that she was beautiful, aged about twenty and with a fine figure.

'What's your name, Miss?' Sam asked her.

'Consuela Martinez,' she told him with a pronounced Mexican accent.

'What were you doing out here?'

'My uncle has a small ranch near the Rio Grande on this side of the border. My father thought it would be safer for me there now that there is war in Mexico. The Apaches came and burned it down. They killed him and took me prisoner but I managed to escape and stole one of their horses.' She paused and looked around anxiously. 'There were three of them, *señor*, but the other one has disappeared.'

'They killed one of my men and stole some horses. The other one probably took the horses back to their camp.'

She nodded and pointed further to the east. 'Their camp is about ten miles from here, I think. I'm not sure how many there are, about fifty perhaps.'

Sam nodded. 'Did they . . . harm you before you escaped?'

Consuela swallowed hard. 'I know what it is you are asking. They captured my aunt also and they started on her first. . . .' Then she collapsed sobbing and Sam gently sat down on the ground with her as she haltingly told him how the poor woman had been raped repeatedly. Consuela could do nothing to help but felt guilty at having taken the chance to get away before becoming her captors' next victim.

Boyd approached them. 'Is everything all right, sir?'

Sam helped Consuela to her feet. 'Miss Martinez has had a lucky escape. We'll take her with us to El

Paso for the time being.'

'What are we going to do about the Apaches? They'll come looking for those two you shot soon enough.'

'There's an abandoned mission a couple of miles west of here, according to the map. I figure we could hole up there and try holding them off until night-fall.'

Boyd nodded. 'It sounds like our best chance, sir. If we press on during the day on foot we'll just get surrounded. Apaches don't attack at night so if we leave the mission at sunset we should make El Paso by dawn.'

'All right, let's get Paterson buried and then fall the men in.'

'Baker and Macdonald are just covering him over now but we thought you'd like to say a few words, sir.'

'Of course, I'll be there in a moment.'

Boyd saluted smartly, tipped his hat to Consuela and strode back towards the men while Sam followed with the girl. He said a brief prayer and talked about Paterson's cheerfulness, love of horses and loyalty to his comrades. Then they set off on foot to the mission where they found crumbling adobe walls, a roofless chapel and the remains of a bell tower. The bell had long since been removed and melted down; the chapel was completely empty but at least they had some shelter and a vantage point from which they could see the enemy's approach.

Sam positioned Svenson, Winters and Macdonald

around the walls and sent Baker up into the bell tower as a lookout. Boyd then approached him to ask what they should do about the prisoners.

'We're going to be heavily outnumbered as it is, sir. If we're to have any chance of holding 'em off we've got to let Fontaine and his men help.'

'He's right, Captain. We've all got the same enemy now,' added the colonel.

'I must have the solemn word of you and your men that you won't attack us or try to escape. You must also agree to surrender those weapons when we set off again at nightfall.'

'You have my word, Captain. My men will follow my orders.'

Sam cut the colonel's bonds before handing over his sword and pistol. 'From now on, your men will take their orders from me as the officer in command. Is that clear?'

Fontaine smiled wryly. 'Until nightfall, Captain, provided we live that long.'

'At least we've an extra three fighters, sir,' said Macdonald.

'Perhaps you'd better make that four.' All heads turned as Consuela spoke. She was holding the rifle that Sam had used earlier and reloading it like an expert. 'I mean no offence, Captain, but I'm a better shot than you. I would never hit a horse if I was aiming at the rider.'

Sam smiled with good humour, despite their predicament. 'No offence has been taken, Miss

Martinez. I just hope for our sake that you really are a better shot than me.'

Corporal Milton took up a position next to Fontaine along the wall while Gates crouched between Winters and Macdonald. Sam, Svenson, Consuela and Boyd spread out further along and they waited tensely for the attack. An hour passed with no sign of any Apaches and then another.

'Where are they?' muttered Sam.

'They're coming all right. They just want to make us sweat for a bit. After all, we ain't goin' no place,' Boyd told him.

Suddenly there was a shout from the bell tower. 'I can see them, Captain!'

'Hold your fire!' Sam ordered as a cloud of dust came into view and then each of them heard the chilling sound of an Apache war cry. The cloud moved rapidly closer until the warriors and their horses became visible. Sam ordered the group to start firing just as they came within range and was pleased to see three Apaches tumble to the ground.

Sam was relieved to see that although a band of more than twenty had come against them, it was not the entire war party. But they were still outnumbered more than three to one. Some were armed with guns but Apache marksmanship with a bow was just as deadly. He heard a cry from up above him and saw Baker tumble to his death from the bell tower after an arrow struck his chest. Consuela spotted the man who had fired it and shot him immediately. The enemy had drawn closer now and bullets and arrows were landing all around them, throwing up dust. Desperately, they returned fire as rapidly as they could to drive the Apaches back from the wall but after falling back briefly they spread themselves out in an effort to surround the mission, searching for gaps in their defences where they could pour through.

'We need some men at the back,' Sam told Boyd.

'Svenson, Macdonald, Milton and Gates! Get to the other side, at the double!' bawled the sergeant and the four men obeyed immediately. As they did so, a warrior on a grey horse cleared the wall behind them. Milton fired and his shot missed but as the Apache raised a spear, the burly corporal pulled him from his horse before caving the man's head in with a rock. He then picked up the spear and hurled it at another Apache, who fell to the ground with a choked cry. Svenson shot a third man but was then hit in the throat by an arrow. A second one went straight through Macdonald's heart as he raised his pistol. Milton picked up the dead man's gun and fired rapidly, a revolver in each hand, as more Apaches tried to get in through the back. One of the dead Apaches had been carrying a rifle and Gates used this to good effect in helping his comrade to hold the others off.

Meanwhile, the others continued to fight off the remaining warriors at the front wall of the mission. There were gaps in the defences, however, and two

Apaches broke through. The first one headed toward Sam, who fired as he swung his body in an arc, hitting his target in the face. Fontaine swung his sword at the other, slashing his chest, and the man tumbled to the ground with a scream. The colonel then thrust the point straight through the wounded Apache's heart as Winters shot another man wielding a tomahawk. Suddenly the enemy withdrew, galloping off in a cloud of dust.

'Are they retreating?' Sam asked Boyd.

'I doubt it. They're probably just regrouping for another assault.' The sergeant had fought Apaches and other tribes many times during his twenty years of service and Sam had no reason to doubt what he was being told.

A hot wind blew a tumbleweed across his path, giving the captain an idea. He seized it and told the others to gather any bits of shrub they could find before the enemy returned. As they did so, Sam explained that he planned to build a firewall to scare the horses and hold the Apaches back. Then Fontaine pointed to the ruined chapel where a few rafters remained from what had once been the roof.

'Milton, go get those pieces of wood!' he shouted and the corporal ran to do his bidding. Within minutes, they had surrounded the outer wall with a barrier of wood, shrubs, cloth and weeds, which Fontaine liberally soaked with brandy from the flask he carried with him. Boyd had a fondness for cigars and decided that this would be a good time to smoke his last one. As he did so, they waited tensely and within moments the Apaches returned. There were now about a dozen warriors left but with two of their own men dead, the odds remained heavily stacked against them.

This time, their enemies went for a full frontal assault so Milton and Gates hurried forward to take up new positions. Again, they faced a hail of arrows and bullets, frequently ducking down below the wall to avoid being killed. They were getting low on ammunition and the strength of the attack made it difficult to shoot accurately, preventing them from hitting any of their assailants. Sam doubted that they could hold out much longer and prayed that his plan would work. At last, the enemy came near enough and Boyd threw his smoking cigar onto one of the brandy-soaked brambles. The flames leaped high and quickly spread over the scattered wood and vegetation as the liquor provided a potent fuel.

The horses reared in terror, two of them throwing their riders while the others struggled to regain control of their mounts. Sam and his companions were able to shoot at them over the flames with little in the way of return fire. Three more fell dead to the ground but then, as Gates foolishly stood up on the wall to improve his aim, an arrow whizzed past, cutting his cheek. He fell back as blood ran from the wound. Nevertheless, the enemy was now in disarray and Sam watched with satisfaction as they retreated.

'It's about an hour until sunset,' Boyd commented. 'My guess is they'll go back to camp and come back in full force at first light with the aim of wiping us out.'

'I hope you're right. In any case we'll bury the dead, get a couple of hours' rest and set off when it's dark.' Sam looked at the devastation that surrounded them, sick of battles and all they entailed. He was due to leave the army in a month's time and a sense of relief flooded through him as the realization dawned that he had probably seen his last battle.

CHAPTER TWO

'Your men fought well,' Sam told Fontaine.

The colonel nodded. 'Perhaps you could show your appreciation by letting us go. If you told your commanding officer the Apaches killed us all, he'd be none the wiser and we could slip across the border into Mexico.'

Sam shook his head. 'I'm sorry but I've got my orders. As a soldier you ought to understand that.'

Fontaine smiled wryly. 'You refused to salute me, Captain, on the grounds that I'm no longer an officer. As you said, the war's over so why not let us go?'

'It seems to me the war is only over when it suits you. Until yesterday you and your men were prepared to carry on fighting and you're going to have to answer for that.'

At that moment, seeking to defuse the situation, Consuela approached Gates with a handkerchief, which she held against the cut on his cheek. Seeing a chance to turn the tables, Gates grabbed her and rammed the muzzle of his revolver against the side of her head. Fontaine calmly cocked his own weapon and Milton did the same.

'Well done, Gates,' Fontaine said without taking his eyes off Sam. 'Now, Captain, order your men to throw their weapons down or Miss Martinez will lose that pretty head of hers. You have precisely ten seconds to decide.'

'You wouldn't!' gasped Boyd.

'I assure you, Sergeant, that I will give the order and Gates will carry it out.' Then the colonel added mockingly, 'As a soldier you ought to understand that.'

Sam reluctantly dropped his gun and signalled to Boyd and Winters that they should do the same. Milton stepped forward to collect their weapons but as he bent down, Consuela sank her teeth into Gates's hand so that the soldier howled with pain and loosened his grip. His gun went off as they struggled and he slumped to the ground as a bullet tore through his chest, leaving powder burns as well as a rapidly spreading bloodstain. Sam kicked Milton under the chin as the corporal turned to see the commotion behind him and fell back sprawling in the sand. Fontaine was momentarily distracted by the death of Gates, and Boyd took the opportunity to pick up his weapon and shoot the colonel's pistol out of his hand. By the time Milton was on his feet, Winters was pointing a revolver at him.

Consuela ran to Sam and he put an arm around her as she buried her head in his shoulder. He did not avert his gaze from Fontaine, however, and saw that the colonel's eyes blazed with fury.

'Since you choose to behave like common criminals, you'll be treated as such,' Sam told him. Then he ordered Boyd to supervise Fontaine and Milton as they dug the graves and buried the dead. Consuela prepared a meal of dried beef and beans from their meagre provisions and once they had eaten the two remaining prisoners' hands were bound. Winters guarded them as they rested for a couple of hours and then they set off on the journey to El Paso with a full moon to light their way.

It was a cold, hungry and footsore band of stragglers who reached the military post as the first streaks of dawn appeared in the sky. Boyd shivered as he pulled his tunic more closely around him. 'Damned desert, it's like a furnace during the day and then Alaska when night falls. I wish the sun would come up.'

'You'll be warm soon enough, Sergeant, when you get some hot coffee inside you. Then we can all get some sleep.' Sam told him.

'Why have we been brought here, Captain?' Fontaine asked.

'I'm just following General Sheridan's orders. As long as there's a cell to put you in, that's all I care about.'

Boyd grinned wolfishly as he pushed the prisoners

forward. 'I wish we could hang 'em both now, sir. I'd sure like to hear Fontaine whistle a rebel song from the end of a rope.'

It was growing lighter as the sentry let them in through the gate. The military post had been burned down during the war but some effort had been made to rebuild the blackened walls. It was clear that much of the roofing had been restored but there was a great deal of work left to do.

'General Sheridan will be visiting this morning, sir. He left orders that you're to see him as soon as you've rested,' the sentry told him.

'I'll do that. In the meantime, is there anywhere for Miss Martinez to bathe, change her clothes and rest for a while? She's had quite an ordeal.'

'I'll show you where the officers' maids have their quarters. You'll be quite comfortable there, miss,' the sentry told Consuela.

Boyd marched the prisoners over to the punishment block where they could be safely locked up while Sam made his way to the officers' quarters. An orderly prepared a bathtub for him and took his soiled uniform away to be cleaned. Then, after a breakfast of ham and eggs, he sank gratefully into clean sheets and slept for several hours. When Sam awoke, his uniform had been returned and his boots polished. He dressed quickly and left the spartan quarters, stepping out into the bright sunshine. The military post at El Paso was now a hive of activity with soldiers engaged in various tasks to repair the damaged buildings. The only sounds were those of saws, hammers and orders being shouted.

A corporal approached him and saluted smartly. 'General Sheridan sends his compliments, sir, and would like to see you right away.'

Sam followed him up a flight of stone steps to a rectangular wood and sandstone building, which the general was using as his quarters. He was shown in to see Sheridan's tiny frame hunched over a desk littered with papers amongst which was a large map. Sam saluted and the general looked up sharply before gesturing for him to sit down on a hard wooden chair.

'I've heard Sergeant Boyd's report. It seems you did the best job you could under the circumstances.' Sheridan sat back and tugged the end of his long black moustache thoughtfully. 'I like the way you saw off those Apaches. Very imaginative.'

'Thank you, sir.'

Sheridan hunched forward again and clasped his hands in front of him on the desk. 'Well, I'll come straight to the point now, Curtis. The two men you brought back have particular skills I need. Fontaine is completely fluent in both French and Spanish. He worked in Mexico before the war for a firm which imported agricultural machinery and knows the country like the back of his hand. Milton is something of a genius with explosives, having been a mining engineer—'

'Excuse me, sir, but I'm completely confused.'

Sheridan chuckled. 'Yes, of course you are. I expect you thought I wanted to make an example of those men to discourage further resistance, eh?'

Sam nodded. 'Yes, sir, but it seems you have something else in mind.'

'You're damned right I do.' The general spread a map out on the table between them. 'The situation in Mexico has now reached a crisis point. The deposed president, Benito Juarez, has fled to Chihuahua City. Emperor Maximilian has forty thousand French troops at his disposal plus some Belgians and Royalist Mexican soldiers. The Mexican Republican Army is scattered, fighting a guerrilla war against the invaders.'

Sam frowned. 'I don't understand, sir. What does this have to do with Fontaine?'

'I'm getting to that. President Jackson doesn't want Europeans interfering with democratically elected governments on our borders. We kicked the British out to win our freedom and now we've got to help the Mexicans do the same. That's why I've been dropping arms over the border for the rebel forces to collect. We don't recognize Maximilian as the rightful ruler of Mexico and we never will.'

Sam groaned inwardly. He had the uneasy feeling that Sheridan was about to involve him in some harebrained scheme to impress the politicians in Washington.

'Now, we have a new challenge, here, about a hundred miles from Mexico City,' Sheridan continued as he jabbed his forefinger at a point on the map. Sam peered at it with growing unease.

'Tacambaro. Wasn't there a battle there?'

The general nodded. 'The rebels occupied the town after driving out the Belgian troops. Strategically, it's very important but they need more weapons if they're to keep it.'

'Transporting weapons hundreds of miles through French held territory will take weeks and we can't send soldiers all that way into Mexico without starting a war.'

Sheridan slammed his hand down on to the desk. 'That's right! So, here's the plan. I've got three wagonloads of rifles, pistols, ammunition and explosives to send to Tacambaro. Now, in order to shore up his support, Maximilian has offered land to ex-confederates who want to settle in Mexico. His troops don't regard southerners with suspicion and Fontaine could easily pose as someone importing machinery like he used to. The weapons will all be hidden underneath it.'

Sam shook his head. 'You can't trust either him or Milton, sir. Once over the border, they'll run off the first chance they get.'

'I've no doubt they would, without an incentive.' Sheridan held up two documents. 'These are amnesties for both Fontaine and Milton, pardoning them for all offences committed since the surrender and signed by me in my capacity as military commander of the south west district. Once you've added

29

your signature, they are free men. They'll also get five hundred dollars each to help them get started again upon their return.'

'They might be tempted by an offer like that,' Sam conceded with some reluctance.

'As a matter of fact, they've already agreed. I want you to go with them, taking Boyd and Winters to back you up. You'll be wearing civilian clothes, of course, and posing as Fontaine's employees. You're the man in charge, though, and it's up to you to make sure that those weapons get delivered. Is that understood?'

Realizing that he had no choice in the matter, Sam stood up and saluted. 'Yes, sir.'

'Very well, Captain. That will be all.' Sheridan then handed him a sheaf of documents. 'You'll need these. You leave first thing tomorrow.'

Sam stepped outside and looked through the papers Sheridan had provided. There was a forged order for steam locomotive parts by the Imperial Mexican Railway Company and documents relating to an engineering firm, which listed Fontaine as its representative. The amnesty papers were in a separate envelope along with a wad of pesos to cover their expenses. Someone had clearly been to a lot of trouble to make the cover story convincing but smuggling weapons through miles of hostile territory during a civil war was highly dangerous, no matter what the precautions.

Sam glanced over to his left and saw that Boyd and

Winters were checking the contents of a wagon and arranging some pieces of heavy machinery on top. Both men jumped down and saluted Sam as he came across to them.

'At ease,' he told them. 'Has General Sheridan given you your orders?'

Boyd nodded. 'I was locking Fontaine up when he arrived this morning, sir.'

'Then you know what we're up against.'

The sergeant rubbed his cleft chin thoughtfully. 'We might not have much of a chance but if anyone can pull this off, you can.'

'Thanks, Sergeant. I'm glad you and Winters are coming along. At least I'll have two men I know I can rely on.'

'We won't let you down, sir,' Winters assured him.

'Neither will I,' said a female voice behind him.

Sam turned around and was surprised to see Consuela standing there. She had bathed and changed into a blouse and riding breeches, her hair was tied under a black hat, which she wore cocked at an angle.

'Miss Martinez, I thought you would be resting.'

'There'll be time to rest when Mexico is free, Captain. In the meantime, I look forward to our journey tomorrow.'

'I don't know what you've been told, Miss Martinez, but I can't take any passengers when I leave here with my men. I shall be on military business and my duties involve some danger,' Sam told her sternly.

31

Consuela's mouth twisted in a grimace. 'It obviously has not occurred to you that I might be of some assistance.'

'To be honest, it hadn't,' he replied bluntly. 'Our work is dangerous and taking a woman along would just be an added complication.'

'I see.' Consuela's tone was icily polite. 'Well, here's another complication for you, Captain: my father, Manuel Martinez, was a congressman and a close friend of President Juarez. Now he is a political prisoner because he refused to accept the new regime and our foreign emperor. I'm in touch with some of the rebels and am familiar with their hideouts. I know my country better than you do and I know I can help.'

Sam shook his head. 'I'm sorry but it's too dangerous. General Sheridan would never agree.'

Consuela smiled then. 'Oh, but he has done so already. Last year, I came to Washington with my father to appeal for help resisting the invaders. I met the general and when I saw him again this morning, he remembered me. He was only too pleased to accept my offer of help when I told him about my contact with the rebel forces.'

'He said nothing about it to me!' protested Sam.

'It was meant to be a pleasant surprise,' she told him petulantly. 'I asked General Sheridan to let me be the one to tell you. Obviously, I made a mistake.' Then she turned on her heel and walked away while Sam stared after her.

'Somehow, I don't think that this is going to be a pleasant trip,' said Winters ruefully.

The rest of the day was taken up with preparations for their departure, then Sam retired early for the night but slept only fitfully. He had hoped for a month of light duties before returning to civilian life but now he faced a dangerous mission in partnership with two former enemies he could not trust. He was angry with himself for upsetting Consuela who only wanted to help but now felt rebuffed by his insensitivity. Sam sighed heavily as dawn broke and reluctantly got up to face the day ahead.

The grey shirt, jeans and duster he put on were what any civilian might wear. The gun-belt and riding boots fitted him snugly and his black hat had a broad brim. Boyd, Winters and Milton were similarly attired but Fontaine wore a blue suit with a matching derby hat, as befitted someone posing as a successful businessman. He stood there smiling, looking quite the dandy with his thumbs in his waistcoat pockets, and watched while the others loaded the wagons with the last of their provisions.

'Give them a hand, Fontaine,' Sam told him.

'I don't think that would do at all. You're supposed to be working for me, aren't you? Besides, it would be a shame to spoil these nice clothes.'

'Let's get one thing straight,' Sam told him. 'We only pretend when we have to. The rest of the time, you and Milton will take your orders from me and Sergeant Boyd. Do I make myself clear?'

Fontaine sighed with mock exasperation. 'A gentleman doesn't need to throw his weight around, Curtis. Why don't you ask nicely and I'll consider your request.'

The ex-colonel was not expecting the blow when it came and Sam's fist sent him sprawling in the dirt as it connected neatly with his jaw. Milton immediately jumped down from the wagon and stood between them.

'What's the matter? Can't your boss stand up for himself?' Sam asked coolly.

Milton's hand hovered near his holster and Sam got ready to draw. By this time, Fontaine was on his feet, wiping a trickle of blood from the corner of his mouth.

'Don't be a fool, Corporal,' he hissed. 'If you shoot him it's the end for both of us!'

Milton reluctantly went back to his duties while Fontaine stood dusting himself down. When he had finished he shot Sam a look of pure hatred but said nothing.

'I gave you an order, Fontaine. Step out of line too many times and I might be forced to shoot you. You see, I don't give a rat's ass about your amnesty so from now on you'd better just do as I say.'

Realizing that Sam was serious, Fontaine turned away and started to load the last two boxes before securing them on the front wagon and climbing up on to the passenger seat. Boyd ordered Winters to take the reins beside Fontaine; he drove the second wagon himself and told Milton to drive the third. Sam approved of these arrangements, thinking it wise to keep their enemies separated. Consuela then arrived and prepared to climb on to the second wagon beside Boyd. Sam approached her cautiously.

'I'm sorry about what I said yesterday. I was just concerned for your safety.'

Consuela broke into a smile. 'Let's just forget about it. Besides, I know I can get a bit high and mighty sometimes.'

'There's a pinto in the stables if you want to use him. You can ride up in front with me if you like.'

She smiled more broadly then. 'Yes, I'd like that very much.'

Then Sam smiled too. Perhaps this mission would turn out well after all.

When they left El Paso they crossed a wooden bridge over the Rio Grande and then reached the rebel-held town of El Paso del Norte, nestled between two mountain ranges which rose out of the desert before them. The sun climbed above the peaks like a red eye opening beneath a heavy lid as the cool dawn gave way to the heat of the day. Beyond the town, the desert stretched ahead of them, an arid landscape which, though it held a certain stark beauty, seemed pitilessly indifferent to their fate.

The town consisted of narrow, dusty streets and low adobe buildings. It was quiet at this hour, the only sounds being those made by goats and chickens in the inhabitants' back yards. Then, ahead of them, Sam saw a tightly knit group of men riding slowly towards them. Several were mounted on mules but the man in front rode a dappled mare. As they approached the men blocking their way, a voice called out to them to stop.

'That's far enough, *gringos,* any closer and we'll shoot!'

Sam held up his right hand, signalling to his companions that they should obey, and they drew to a halt. The man riding in front continued to approach, his followers keeping pace just behind him. He held the reins firmly in his left hand and a pistol in his right while staring purposefully ahead. Sam noticed that the Mexican wore a bandolier across his chest over a faded, military tunic, which had several buttons missing. A shapeless peaked cap was pushed back from his head and a mass of curly black hair flowed beneath it. A moustache bristled under his squat nose and his features were coarse and unshaven. He drew to a halt just inches away and his men, who appeared similarly armed and dressed in a mixture of peasant clothes and items of uniform, gathered around him.

'I am Captain Pedro Mendoza of the Mexican Republican Army and these are my men. What are you *gringos* doing here?'

CHAPTER THREE

'Good morning, Captain. We are travelling on business but perhaps I should let my employer explain,' said Sam in a conciliatory tone.

Mendoza nodded and Sam called Fontaine down from his wagon. The former colonel strode confidently up to Mendoza and addressed him politely in Spanish. The two men exchanged words briefly but it was Consuela who translated the content for Sam.

'Captain Mendoza is suspicious and wants to see some documentation.'

Sam passed Fontaine the forged order form and engineered company papers. Mendoza peered at them for what seemed like a long time and appeared very displeased. Finally, he addressed them once more in English.

'So, you are enemies of Mexico. You come here to help Maximilian build trains so he can move his troops around the country.'

'We're just helping to develop your country, sir.

The trains will be for civilians to use. The Republic of Mexico will need a railway system, won't it?' protested Fontaine.

Mendoza's eyes narrowed suspiciously. 'You are from the Southern states, no? All you confederates support Maximilian because he gives you land – our land.'

'I assure you we are completely neutral and pose no threat to you or your men.'

Mendoza smiled then. 'Very well, we will search your wagons thoroughly. If it is as you say, there will only be parts for a steam train. If we find weapons, you all die, including the *señorita* there, since she betrays her people.'

Then Consuela spoke rapidly in Spanish and Mendoza's eyes widened in surprise. He turned and looked questioningly at Sam. 'So now we have a different story, eh? You're really on our side!'

'It's true, Captain,' Sam assured him. 'You've got to believe us. We're travelling to Tacambaro with weapons for your comrades holding the fort. You must let us through!'

Mendoza conferred briefly with his subordinates and then spoke once more. 'It may be as you say so, instead of killing you, we will let you go back across the border in return for giving us the weapons.'

Sam shook his head firmly. 'I can't agree to those terms. My orders from General Sheridan were very clear. These arms are to be used to hold Tacambaro for President Juarez. Don't you realize how important that is? It's less than a hundred miles from Mexico City!'

'General Sheridan is not in command here!' bawled Mendoza. 'My men can make good use of those weapons. It is we who fight and die for Mexico, not you *gringos!*'

'I've got armed men behind me too, Mendoza. Don't force us to fight you,' said Sam.

Mendoza chuckled and then gave a loud whistle. At that moment, over a dozen men armed with rifles appeared on the rooftops surrounding them.

'For God's sake, give them the goddamn weapons and let's get out of here!' hissed Fontaine desperately. Sam did not reply and there was a tense moment while he considered his next move. He was about to conclude that surrender was their only option when a new arrival pushed his way through Mendoza's men and stood between the two groups. He was a short, stocky individual, dressed in a dark suit and string tie. His bald, dome-shaped head was surrounded by a fringe of iron-grey hair which matched his beard. The man looked like a lawyer or an academic of some sort and seemed out of place in these surroundings as he looked up at Mendoza through round, wire-framed spectacles. The two exchanged a brief conversation in Spanish and Sam noticed that the captain adopted a respectful tone while speaking. Then the man turned to face Sam and his eyes widened in surprise as he looked at Consuela. She too gasped in astonishment and immediately jumped down from her horse to embrace him. The two smiled and chattered excitedly for a few moments while the others looked on, dumbfounded.

'Would someone mind telling me just what is going on?' demanded Sam.

'This is Manuel Martinez, my father!' Consuela told him excitedly. 'Now we are truly safe.'

Mendoza immediately ordered his men to stand down and he put his own pistol away. 'Forgive me. Had we known you were travelling with Señorita Martinez, you would have had no trouble from us.'

Martinez then turned to face Sam. 'My daughter tells me you saved her life. I will be forever in your debt, Captain Curtis.'

'It seems you've saved us all today, sir, and I thank you in return.'

'Think nothing of it. I escaped from prison two weeks ago and have been in hiding here. This is the first chance I have had to do something for the Revolution. Now I must go to Chihuahua City where President Juarez has his headquarters. Might I have the honour of travelling that far with you?'

'You can do so with pleasure, sir. In fact, your presence may prove useful should we run into any more of your friends,' Sam told him.

Within a few minutes, Martinez was mounted on a horse and bidding goodbye to Mendoza whose men now parted to let them through. Once through the town, they picked their way through the narrow pass ahead and journeyed on into the desert. Sam rode beside Boyd's wagon for a while, leaving Consuela to become re-acquainted with her father.

'That was a close one back there, sir,' remarked Boyd.

'You're right there. It looks like Lady Luck's on our side today.'

'I wouldn't be too sure about that,' said the sergeant drily, nodding over to his right.

Sam followed his glance and spotted the smoke signals in the distance. His heart sank as he realized what had happened.

'Apaches don't give up easy,' said Boyd, as if reading his thoughts. 'It makes sense, I guess. They'll have picked up our trail when we left that old mission, decided not to risk an attack at El Paso but to wait until we were on our own out in the desert.'

'We don't stand much chance out here,' said Sam. Then he had a sudden thought. 'Which box contains the explosives?'

Boyd jerked a thumb behind him. 'There's a box of nitroglycerine at the bottom of the wagon Milton's driving.'

'I can see a rocky outcrop up ahead. Head for that and I'll talk to Milton. Don't say anything about what we've seen until we get there. I don't want any panic.'

Boyd nodded and Sam dropped back until he was riding beside Milton's wagon. 'I hear you're good with explosives. Can you handle nitroglycerine?'

'Sure I can. There are some bottles of nitro in the

back there. I packed them in sand to keep the stuff cool and stop it from blowing us all up.'

'Good. When we reach those rocks up ahead, you're to get that nitroglycerine out and prepare to use it.'

'I guess we've got trouble then,' said Milton grimly. 'Those Apaches are back again.'

'Damn, I thought we'd lost them.'

Soon they reached the rocks and drew the wagons in behind them. Sam helped Milton locate the crate of nitroglycerine and quickly forced open the lid with his knife. As Milton carefully removed some bottles of the oily liquid, Sam peered through his telescope and saw that the Apaches were now approaching.

'They're still far off but heading this way, so we don't have much time.'

Milton cut some lengths of rope to make fuses and asked Sam to help him. The two of them then moved out a short distance from the rocks just within range of fire and buried several bottles they had opened in sand, trailing rope fuses from them back towards the rocks. Sam followed Milton's instructions, realizing that the explosive they were using was highly unstable, particularly when it was unpacked.

By the time they returned, Boyd had got the others sheltered behind rocks in strategic positions, armed with rifles. Sam settled down beside Martinez, leaving Milton to see to the fuses. The remaining bottles were packed in the crate but could quickly be removed and thrown at the enemy. Sam knew that they would explode on impact.

'I'm sorry to have led you into danger, sir,' Sam told Martinez.

The older man smiled. 'In Mexico these days, none can avoid danger, Captain.'

Finally, they heard the chilling war cry of the Apaches and the warriors came into view. This time they were more than thirty strong, riding hard towards them. Milton lit the fuses at intervals and the first explosion occurred as the enemy came within range. There was a deafening roar and sand burst up into the air as men were thrown from their horses. Sam ordered them to start firing as the smoke cleared and several more Apaches tumbled to the ground. However, the others quickly regrouped and returned fire as they headed once more in Sam's direction.

'I reckon we must have got about a dozen of them,' said Winters as an arrow whizzed past his ear.

'That just leaves a ratio of three to one then,' remarked Fontaine drily as he let off another shot. Bullets and arrows now ricocheted off the rocks in front of them and they huddled lower to avoid being hit. Then there was a second explosion but the Apaches had shifted their angle of attack slightly and only four of them were killed by it. However, as they re-grouped, it was quickly followed by a third explosion which flung men and horses from the middle of the war party up into the air. The ground was now littered with bloodied corpses but there were still ten Apaches left.

Their chief was clearly visible in his headdress, directing his braves to spread themselves out more rather than attempt a full frontal assault. The Apaches were getting closer now, working their way in from the sides and they moved their own positions accordingly. Two horsemen galloped towards them from the right and Boyd swung quickly in an arc, shooting them both. Winters suddenly gave a cry of pain and slumped forward with an arrow between his shoulders. Sam was on his back in a split second and fired at the warrior who had approached from behind the wagons, the bullet hitting the man neatly between the eyes. He saw another climb up to drive one of the wagons away and shot him in the stomach.

Fontaine dodged a blow from a tomahawk and shot the thrower dead while Milton threw one of the bottles of nitroglycerine at the remaining Apaches. Unfortunately, it landed too far away and none were killed but their horses reared in terror and one man was thrown off. Consuela shot him as he tried to get back on his mount. There were now four Apaches left, including the chief, and Milton still had one bottle of nitroglycerine. As he reached down to get it, an arrow pierced his shoulder and he stumbled to the side. Martinez ran forward to get the bottle while the others covered him. He seized it and drew back his arm to throw but took too long taking aim in his exposed position. The chief shot him squarely in the chest and he slumped forward, throwing the bottle as he did so. It landed short of the target and exploded harmlessly.

Consuela screamed as she watched her father fall and, heedless of the danger to herself, ran over to him while Sam and the others were exchanging fire with the remaining Apaches. The chief then galloped forward, seizing Consuela's hair as she bent over her father's body. Sam turned as she was being pulled up on to the chief's horse and squeezed his trigger only to hear the click of an empty chamber. With no time to reload, he ran forward with a roar, wielding the rifle like a club. It smashed into the chief's body and he tumbled to the ground, releasing Consuela as he did so. Sam then brought the butt of his weapon crashing down on the chief's skull.

The remaining three Apaches, seeing their chief and the rest of their comrades dead, turned and fled. Fontaine stood and fired after them, killing one and injuring a second.

'There's no call for that,' Boyd told him. 'They were no longer any threat to us.'

'There was no call for you Yankees to go burning your way through the South but you still did it. Now you expect me to give quarter to savages when you wouldn't spare the lives and property of honest Christians.'

'A lot of things happened during the war that I didn't agree with but that don't make what you just did right. Besides, I had a brother who died in

Andersonville where a lot of honest Christians died of disease and starvation. Are you gonna defend that?'

Fontaine shrugged but said nothing. Then he went over to Milton to tend his comrade's wound. The arrow had not penetrated very deeply but Milton grimaced with pain as it was removed. Consuela then offered her shawl to use as a bandage.

'You did well with that nitroglycerine,' Sam told the injured corporal as he was being fixed up.

'Yeah, sorry about Martinez and Winters. I guess everybody fought hard today.'

Consuela went back and knelt down by her father's body, holding his lifeless hand in hers while the tears ran down her cheeks. Sam put a hand on her shoulder and squeezed gently, not knowing what to say to comfort her.

'Only an hour ago I was overjoyed to see him but it was to be for the last time.'

'He was a very brave man; you should be proud of him.'

She nodded. 'I am. Will you help me to bury him?'

Sam fetched two spades from the wagon and they laid Martinez to rest with Winters beside him. Then they hitched up the wagons once more and headed southwest, going deeper into the desert towards their eventual destination. Weeks of travel through rough terrain lay ahead so Sam dismissed from his mind all thoughts of the dangers they had already encountered. He could only hope that their journey proceeded more smoothly from now on.

'Are we likely to encounter any troops in this area?' he asked Consuela.

'The republican forces or Juaristas are mainly a guerrilla army like Mendoza and his men. They fight in this area against the contra-guerrillas but the bulk of the French forces are further south.'

'Who are these contra-guerrillas?'

Consuela grimaced. 'A bunch of mercenaries from different countries commanded by a French colonel, Dupin. They're quite vicious and the people hate them.'

'Let's hope we don't meet any.'

She shrugged. 'I shouldn't worry. They won't harm us as long as they don't find out what we are really doing here.'

At that moment, Fontaine's wagon drew alongside them and he showed Sam a route he had marked out on the map. 'We should reach the edge of this desert in about ten days. I suggest we head for Victoria de Durango where we can change horses and pick up fresh supplies.'

'There are French troops in Durango, aren't there?' said Sam.

'There are French troops in a lot of places. That's why we have those documents and the locomotive parts.'

'I guess so. It would look suspicious if we kept trying to avoid them. What do you think, Consuela?'

'What Mr Fontaine says makes sense,' she conceded.

47

Sam handed the map back. 'All right, Fontaine. We'll do as you suggest.'

'As long as it's all right with Miss Martinez, you mean,' replied the southerner resentfully.

'You'll get that amnesty if you do your job but don't expect me to trust you,' Sam told him.

They approached a low-lying range and climbed higher, past clumps of yucca, creosote and mesquite plants. The path was steep but broad enough for the wagons to pass and although their progress was slow, the air was cooler, with grasslands and a few trees to provide shade. As they descended into the valley below, Sam spotted what looked like a church tower and a cluster of buildings.

'There's a village down there where we could stop for the night,' he said.

As they approached, however, there was a whiff of burning and when they entered the village, the reason for it became clear. What had once been people's homes were now reduced to a series of roof-less, blackened stumps. The main street was littered with bloodied corpses, some of them shot, others bayoneted to death. Among them were the bodies of women and children. There was a tree in the main square and a dead man hung from one of its branches, his feet swaying gently in the breeze.

Sam had seen some brutal sights during the war but never anything like this. Consuela covered her face while Boyd and Milton both appeared shocked. Fontaine shrugged as if to say that such things

48

happened in wartime but said nothing. Sam tethered his horse to the tree, climbed up and drew his knife to cut the man down. At that moment, a bullet whizzed over his head and embedded itself in the trunk.

'I wouldn't do that, Monsieur, if I were you.'

They all turned to look at the man who had fired the shot. Sam judged him to be in his fifties with a grey beard that hung over his chest. He was clad in a black sombrero and a bright red dolman festooned with medals and was mounted on an impressive black horse with a white streak on its forehead.

'He's dead. Isn't that punishment enough for whatever he's done?' Sam asked.

The bearded man smiled. 'He is to hang there until he rots and the vultures peck his eyes out. This will warn others to obey their emperor and refuse help to bandits like him.'

'Those women and children we saw, are they a warning too?' asked Boyd.

The bearded man spread his arms expansively. 'It is regrettable, of course, but what can I do? These peasants insist on giving food and shelter to the Juaristas. Their daughters sleep with them and their sons join them in the hills to fight. This is the only way to prevent such things.'

Sam climbed down from the tree, looked more closely at the man's uniform, taking in the decorations and the French accent. 'Are you Colonel Dupin?'

'Ah, I see you know me!' Dupin swept off his hat

and gave a low bow. 'Who, may I ask, are you?'

'I'm Sam Curtis. I work for Mr Fontaine over there who has all our papers.'

Fontaine handed over the documentation and the colonel studied it for a moment before nodding his approval. 'Well, at least you all seem to be on the right side but it is fortunate that you ran into me. This area is crawling with rebels so I'll escort you to safety.'

Throughout this conversation, Consuela continued to sob quietly and Dupin cantered forward to speak to her. 'My dear Mademoiselle, whatever is the matter?'

'I think the lady is distressed by the sight of this man left hanging here.'

Dupin sighed reluctantly. 'Very well, Monsieur. You may cut him down. Then please follow me to the cantina where some food and drink awaits you.'

Sam reluctantly prepared to follow their host along the street, hoping that their stay would be a brief one.

CHAPTER FOUR

Milton and Boyd saw to the wagons and horses while the others stepped through the batwing doors into the cantina. It was full of Dupin's men who were carousing, swigging from bottles and fondling the dishevelled-looking young women, who reluctantly served them. A thin, weasel-faced individual in a grimy apron stood behind the bar, wiping it nervously.

'Alfredo, bring more tortillas and some stew with a bottle of wine for our new guests!' demanded Dupin and the bartender scurried away to do his bidding. The Frenchman led them over to a quiet table in the corner where an officer sat with a glass of wine and a half-eaten plate of stew in front of him.

'This is Captain Jefferson Slade, one of my best officers,' said Dupin.

Slade looked up at them and his pale blue eyes widened in surprise when he saw Fontaine. 'Well, I do declare, Colonel, this is indeed a pleasant surprise.'

'Captain Slade was one of my best officers, too, and we served together for three years before he became an adjutant to General Lee,' explained Fontaine.

'Well, what brings y'all to Mexico?' asked Slade as they sat down.

'I've gone back into business and I'm importing some machine parts for the Imperial Mexican Railway Company. Do you remember Corporal Milton?'

'Sure I do. That man's some soldier.'

Fontaine nodded. 'He's working for me now.' Then he introduced Sam and Consuela. Slade nodded briefly in Sam's direction but showed far more interest in Consuela. He brushed a hand through his wavy blond hair before flashing an even set of pearl-white teeth in a smile. 'Had I known I was to be treated to such delightful company I would have made myself more presentable,' he told her.

'You're too kind, Captain,' she responded politely.

Dupin clamped a plump cigar between his lips and lit it. 'I should warn you, Mademoiselle, that Captain Slade has quite a reputation with the ladies.'

'I fear Miss Martinez will be unjustly alarmed, sir,' said Slade with mock innocence.

'I can assure the captain that his presence has no effect on me at all,' replied Consuela coolly, a response which met with a chuckle from Dupin.

Milton and Boyd joined them at that point and then their food was served. Sam remained quiet while Fontaine, Milton and Slade reminisced about their wartime experiences. Eventually, Slade turned to Boyd and Sam, asking them what they had done during the war.

'I was a captain in the Union Army and Boyd here was a sergeant under my command' replied Sam, thinking it best to stick as closely to the truth as he could.

'Well, I never thought I'd see the day when Henry Fontaine would employ Yankees, let alone sit down to eat with them.'

'Times change, Captain, and the war's over now,' replied Boyd.

'Well that's easy for you to say, not being among the losers. Some folks, including myself, have lost everything they own,' replied Slade bitterly.

Boyd removed his eye patch and Slade flinched at the sight of the wound. 'We all lost things, Captain. Let's just leave it at that.'

'Come, gentlemen. Now we are all on the same side and with new enemies to fight,' said Dupin as he poured them some more wine.

'We do indeed,' declared Slade as he raised his glass and proposed a toast to 'Soldiers of fortune everywhere'. It was not a sentiment with which Sam could agree but he joined in to preserve the fragile peace. As the evening wore on they grew tired and Dupin showed them to some rooms upstairs where they could spend the night. As they reached the upper floor, however, Slade laid a hand on his former comrade's shoulder. 'Come, Colonel. I've got some brandy in my quarters. Let's drink one last toast to the good ol' boys we left in the ground before you turn in for the night.'

'Very well,' said Fontaine. 'After all, there's no telling when we'll meet again and have the chance to talk over old times.'

Sam exchanged a concerned look with Boyd but there was nothing they could do without arousing suspicion. They would just have to hope that Fontaine did not relax too much with his old friend and let something slip. That could land them all in serious trouble. Dismissing such thoughts from his mind, he settled down to sleep on the hard, narrow bed in the sparsely furnished room he shared with Boyd. Exhaustion soon overcame him and he did not awake until sunrise.

Boyd had already dressed and was buckling on his gun-belt. The two men headed downstairs to find the weasel-faced bartender clearing up after the previous night.

'Good morning. Is there any chance of breakfast before we leave?' Sam asked.

'Certainly, *señor*, but Colonel Dupin wants to see you first.' The Mexican pointed towards the door and Sam stepped outside into the sunshine, followed by Boyd, to find that a chilling sight awaited them. More than a dozen of Dupin's men were lined up, aiming rifles at them. Further to the left stood Dupin, calmly smoking a cigar while he chatted to

Fontaine in French. Slade was standing in front of the cantina, a revolver in his hand.

'I trust you slept well, gentlemen. As you may have guessed by now, your little secret is out so the game's up.'

Sam tried in vain to brazen it out. 'Really, Captain. I've no idea what you're talking about. If my employer is up to something—'

'Forget it, Curtis. You can't worm your way out of it that way. Now, both of you take off those gun-belts, very slowly, and toss them over here.'

Sam and Boyd obeyed reluctantly, having no other option for the time being. Fontaine then came over and picked their weapons up. Slade gestured for them to raise their hands and Fontaine then searched Sam, pulling out the amnesty documents and money given to him by General Sheridan.

'The only thing left for you to do is to sign these papers,' Fontaine told him.

'No chance, Fontaine. It doesn't make any difference what you do to me. You're going to remain a fugitive, skulking out here for the rest of your life.'

'I might do something to your friend Boyd, here,' said Fontaine, nonchalantly.

'Don't listen to him, sir. It's probably nothing he won't do anyway.'

Fontaine stepped back, levelling his gun at them both. 'I do have another option,' he added mischievously and then called out 'Bring the woman!'

Then, to his horror, Sam saw Consuela being

dragged between two soldiers before they stopped just a few feet away from him. Fontaine walked up to her and stroked her cheek with the barrel of his revolver.

'Now, what shall I do with you, my dear? Perhaps Slade would like to enjoy your company for a few hours. What do you say?'

Consuela spat in Fontaine's face and he responded by slapping her hard across the cheek. Sam made to run forward but Boyd held him back.

Dupin stepped forward then to address them. 'Here's our offer, gentlemen. Sign those papers and Miss Martinez will be allowed to go free with a horse, food and water. Refuse and she will die alongside you, once my men have finished with her, of course.'

Sam thought for a moment. 'All right, I'll sign. But not until she's ridden out of here and has a head start.'

'I think we can agree to that, Colonel, since Captain Curtis is a man of honour,' remarked Fontaine.

Dupin nodded and ordered one of his men to fetch the pinto Consuela had been riding. As this was being done, Milton came out of the cantina, looking slightly dishevelled as he had drunk a great deal the previous evening.

'The wheel has turned in our favour, Corporal,' Fontaine told him as Milton stared, nonplussed, at the scene before him.

'What's going on, sir?' he asked.

'We're changing sides. Maximilian will pay hand-somely for those guns and give us land into the bargain. Not only that, but with our pardons signed we can return home rich if we want to. All we have to do is dispose of Curtis and Boyd, here.'

Milton shook his head slowly. 'I don't like it. I fought with these men and I gave my word to 'em. I'm not a man who takes his word back or kills men he's promised to stand alongside.'

'Your scruples are a credit to you but you gave your word under duress – to a bunch of Yankees at that,' Fontaine told him.

Milton shook his head once more. 'I'm sorry but I want no part in this.'

Fontaine flushed with rage. 'You goddamn turn-coat! I'll shoot you down like a dog if you don't follow my orders!'

'I saved your life once during the war but I can't go along with you now. Besides, you ain't a colonel any more and don't have rights over me.'

Fontaine calmed down slightly. 'Very well, Milton. I owe you a life so you can leave with the girl but if I ever see you again, you're a dead man.'

Milton turned towards Sam and Boyd. 'I'm sorry I can't do anything for you but I'll take care of Miss Martinez as best I can.'

Sam quickly signed his amnesty and handed it to him. Then, within minutes, Consuela and Milton were mounted on their horses. Consuela turned a tear-stained face to look hopelessly at Sam and Boyd before she and Milton rode off into the distance. Once they were no longer visible, Sam reluctantly signed the treacherous Fontaine's amnesty and waited to see what his fate would be.

He did not have to wait long. Dupin ordered four of his men to dig a couple of pits in the sand in front of the cantina. Then, the two prisoners were ushered forward and made to stand in them while the sand was filled in up to their necks.

'We'll take the wagons to Victoria de Durango and then under military escort to Mexico City,' Dupin told them. 'I'm sure the emperor will be very pleased.' Then he called over a burly sergeant from his troop. 'Take four men and go after Milton and the girl. We don't want those two running into any rebels and telling them about our new weapons.'

'I swear to God you'll be sorry if I ever catch up with you!' shouted Sam struggling in vain against the walls of sand trapping his body.

Fontaine paused in front of them with Slade at his side. 'We'll leave you gentlemen here to enjoy the sunshine.' Then he gave a mock salute before riding off with the column. Sam watched helplessly as the wagons departed under guard but that was now the least of his worries. He and Boyd had been left to die of exposure, guarded by a troop of contra-guerrillas under the command of a lieutenant who lay in wait for any passing Juaristas seeking shelter. There were a few villagers left alive but none dared come to their aid and the soldiers sat around talking, drinking and laying bets on how long their prisoners would survive. As the morning went on, the sun grew hotter and Sam's mouth felt as dry as burnt paper. A breeze blew sand at him which stuck to the sweat on his face like grit in an oyster. He had not realized that it was possible to be this thirsty and, without a hat, he was aware of the intense heat drying and blistering his exposed skin.

After a few hours, the soldiers became bored and dozed in the shade. The weasel-faced bartender came out of the cantina, looked furtively around and then bent down to give them each a cup of water. Sam and Boyd both drank greedily but the man scurried back inside before they could thank him, afraid that one of the soldiers would awake and see him. A few minutes later, Sam heard the sound of galloping hoofs. The lieutenant awoke with a start and ran to the edge of the village. He quickly aimed with his rifle and fired before giving a shout of triumph. The escaping bartender was dead.

'It looks like our last hope of rescue is gone. He was probably going to fetch help,' whispered Boyd hoarsely.

'I wonder if those men Dupin sent have caught up with Consuela and Milton yet.'

'It's probably best not to think about that, sir. There's nothing we can do, is there.'

'No, I guess not,' replied Sam but his mind continued to dwell on images of what could be happening to Consuela at that very moment. Brutal mercenaries like those employed by Dupin were unlikely to allow her a swift and merciful death but the thought of what else they might do was more painful to him than any of his physical torments.

At that moment Consuela was leading Milton up a narrow path that wound through a steep canyon. Their horses struggled with the climb, sending loose rocks tumbling below, but they urged them forward until they reached a plateau surrounded by rocks where they quickly dismounted. Their pursuers were still some distance behind and Consuela hoped that they had not seen them turn off.

'How many of them were there?' she asked Milton, anxiously.

'I counted five.'

'Thank God there was a rifle in that saddle-bag. Pass it to me, will you?'

Consuela flattened herself against the rock and took aim with the weapon Milton handed her. There was a panoramic view of the desert below and soon a group of riders appeared and then drew to a halt, wondering why they could no longer see their quarry. Consuela squeezed the trigger and the fat sergeant immediately fell dead from his horse. She fired a second time and another soldier threw his arms in the air as the bullet hit his chest. The dead man's foot remained caught in his horse's stirrup and it galloped away. The remaining three men quickly retreated in search of cover and disappeared from view.

Milton suddenly froze, a revolver in his hand. 'They've dismounted, probably found the path,' he whispered. They both moved back against the over-hanging rock and waited tensely. There was a slight bend in the path and Milton peered cautiously round it as a black sombrero came into view. Pointing his gun at a downward angle, he fired and the soldier's hands went up to his face as he fell against one of his comrades who tumbled down to the desert below. A shape darted behind them and Milton fired again but this time the bullet ricocheted and missed its target. He cursed softly and ducked back into their hiding place.

For a moment there was silence and then a faint, scuffling sound. The remaining man had decided to climb the rock face in an attempt to reach another plateau above them. If he succeeded, they would be the sitting targets. Milton signalled silently to Consuela and they crept around the corner, moved out to the edge of the path and peered upwards. She aimed her rifle at a pair of legs and fired but the man was already rolling over on to the ledge above them. Then there was another rifle shot and the soldier's body plunged past them to the ground. A moment later, a familiar face peered down at them.

'That was good shooting, *amigos* but not quite good enough,' said Captain Mendoza.

Back at the village, Sam was not sure how much

longer he could hold out. It was well into the afternoon and the temperature was almost forty degrees.
Both he and Boyd had drunk only a cup of water
each all day. Soon they would die with their bodies
left to rot in the sand and be eaten by ants. He was
beginning to think it would be a merciful release
when it happened. His only comfort was that the five
men sent after Consuela and Milton had not yet
returned. Perhaps they had managed to escape
somehow but he held out little hope that they would
find help in time to save them. He heard a faint
groan next to him and realized that Boyd was still
alive but neither man had the strength to talk.

Their guards sat dozing in the shade and the
remaining villagers were all indoors. All was quiet
and there seemed nothing left to do but wait for
death. These thoughts were interrupted suddenly by
a thunder of hoofs. Their captors awoke, startled,
and each one reached for his rifle but Captain
Mendoza and his men vastly outnumbered them and
had the advantage of surprise. The guards fell in a
hail of bullets and, when the smoke had cleared, six
corpses in red lay sprawled on the ground.

Consuela leaped down from her horse and held a
canteen to Sam's parched lips while Milton did the
same for Boyd. They drank greedily before shovels
were fetched to dig them out. Mendoza came and
squatted in front of them while this was being done.

'Tell me, do you know where those red devils have
taken your weapons?'

'Victoria de Durango,' whispered Sam hoarsely. 'From there, French troops will take them to Mexico City.'

'They have to be stopped,' added Boyd weakly, desperation in his tone.

'Don't worry, *amigos*. Dupin doesn't know this desert like I do. We'll cut them off before they reach Victoria de Durango.'

Mendoza's tone was confident but Sam was not so sure. Time was of the essence when the enemy already had such a head start yet the rebels were preparing to make camp. However, he was too weak to protest and allowed himself to be lifted from his prison of sand, assisted to remove his clothes and bathe. Soothing ointment was applied to his burnt skin, he was given more water and then soup was spooned between his lips before he sank between cool sheets into a deep sleep.

The cry of a cockerel awoke him the next morning at sunrise. His clothes had been cleaned and hung over the end of his bed so Sam dressed hurriedly. No sooner was he ready than Consuela entered the room carrying a breakfast tray.

'You should not be out of bed yet!' she scolded him as she put the tray down.

'We've got to get after Dupin. Too much time has been lost already.'

'Captain Mendoza and his men can recover the weapons. You're in no fit state to travel,' she protested.

Sam shook his head. 'It's my responsibility to see that General Sheridan's guns get to Tacambaro. Where's Boyd, anyway?'

Consuela rolled her eyes at him. 'He's in the next room and being just as stubborn as you but neither of you can go anywhere without breakfast. That's an order!'

Sam sighed. 'OK, but we're both out of here as soon as we've eaten.'

He was starving as it happened and the fresh bread, ham, eggs and coffee was just what he needed to start his journey. Outside, Boyd was saddling their horses, his face red and blistered like his own. Consuela insisted that they both put more ointment on while Mendoza looked on, chuckling. Within a few minutes they were on their way, Sam riding with Milton and Consuela.

'I must thank you both for getting help to us like that yesterday. I hoped you'd get away from Dupin's men but I never expected a rescue.'

'You saved me too, remember?' Consuela reminded him

The ex-confederate smiled and extended his hand to shake. 'It's like I said, Captain. When you agree to ride alongside a man you should stick with him.'

Boyd offered his thanks too and he and Milton were soon firm friends, riding together and swapping reminiscences about the war. They made steady progress across the desert but Sam could not see how they were going to overtake the enemy. Galloping forward, he caught up with Mendoza at the head of the column.

'How do you plan to get ahead of Dupin, Captain?' he asked.

'The State of Durango has mountains and forests. There are trails known to few men, which we use to smuggle weapons. That is where we will manage to cut him off. Those guns will never reach the state capital.'

'How long are we going to be in this desert?'

Mendoza smiled. 'It seems an unwelcome place to you, *amigo*, but it yields secrets to those who know the land well. Tomorrow we will reach a path through the mountains and cut two days from our journey.'

Sam felt some reassurance. If all went well, they would end up a day ahead of their quarry instead of a day behind. This seemed to explain the Mexican's relaxed attitude and unhurried pace which, up to now, he had found maddening. They plodded onward through the stark landscape, dotted with desert shrubs and cacti. Sam noticed an evil-looking buzzard perched like an omen of doom upon the branch of a dead tree. He shivered as he recalled the mishaps that had befallen them so far but figured there was no particular reason to expect any more bad luck. At least, that was what he kept telling himself.

CHAPTER FIVE

Their journey was uneventful that day and they made camp at sunset. Mendoza posted sentries and they settled down to a supper of dried beef, beans and biscuits. Sam slept heavily, despite the hard ground and plummeting temperature and Milton had to prod him awake when the sun was up. There was just enough time for coffee and a hurried breakfast once he had shaved and then they were on their way again.

The path through the mountains was narrow, winding and steep but the air grew cooler as they climbed. The walls of rock which rose up on either side of them made a pleasing contrast to the desert plain below. As they continued to climb, Sam began to feel more confident about the possibility of catching up with Dupin and Fontaine. The thought of settling scores brought a grim smile of satisfaction to his face but it quickly vanished.

The shot which echoed around them sent a trooper tumbling from his horse to the plain below.

It was followed by a hailstorm of bullets which Mendoza's men tried to avoid by moving against the rock face and retreating. Nevertheless, more of them were being hit and the horses started to panic. The bullets seemed to fly from all around them but their assailants could not be seen, except for the sun glinting on their rifle barrels and the occasional glimpse of a sombrero. They continued to fire upward in a vain attempt to ward off the attack as they moved further back down the way they had come, eventually finding some shelter.

At last the shooting stopped and a voice called down to them in Spanish. Mendoza shouted back an angry response and Sam asked Consuela, who was huddled behind him, to translate what had been said.

'The men up there are bandits and their leader is called Manuel Hernandez. He says we are surrounded and must give up our guns, horses and anything else we are carrying.'

'I take it Mendoza refused.'

'Of course he did. Those cutthroats will either shoot us or leave us to die with no food and water.'

Sam looked around, up and behind him, searching for some means of escape. It was then that he spotted a tiny cave-like opening, which came up to waist height. Bending down, he peered through it and saw light at the other end.

'What are you doing?' Boyd asked him.

'I think a few of us could squeeze through here

and get up behind them.'

'We can't be sure where that leads too,' warned the sergeant.

'No, but it's worth a try.'

A few of Mendoza's men clustered around him and Consuela asked one of them to tell their captain what Sam had found. Mendoza could then keep the bandit leader talking by pretending to negotiate their surrender while the others launched an attack. Voices continued to be exchanged as Sam, followed by Boyd and four troopers, crawled through the opening to find that it sloped upwards and widened out into a rocky outcrop at the other side. They emerged just below the parapet on which a dozen bandits had positioned themselves, all with their backs to them.

Sam and his companions all fired at once and four of the bandits were dead before the others managed to turn around and draw their weapons. Three more were killed before the rest started shooting and the bullets now flew in all directions. The trooper to Sam's left and another to Boyd's right were both hit in the chest but Sam got the sharp shooter responsible straight between the eyes and he fell back against the rocks. Boyd killed another who was diving for cover. One bandit's pistol was empty and a trooper shot him as he reached for his rifle. There were now only two bandits left, both of whom threw down their guns to surrender. Sam noticed that one of them was more expensively dressed with several rings, gold teeth and braid on his sombrero. He guessed that this was Manuel Hernandez and beckoned him over.

'Please, *señor*, don't kill me I beg you,' begged Hernandez as he crept forward.

'Tell the rest of your men to stand up so we can see them and to throw their weapons down,' Sam ordered him.

The bandit leader nodded and went back up to the edge of the parapet where he shouted to his men on the opposite side of the canyon. Reluctantly, they did as they were told and cast their weapons down to the desert below. Sam then gestured for him to move ahead of them through the passage to the other side.

'The soldiers will kill me,' he said nervously.

Sam shrugged. 'It's up to Captain Mendoza what he decides to do with you.'

'Please, I have gold, *señor*.' Hernandez sank to his knees as he held out a purse from which coins and items of jewellery spilled on to the rocks at Sam's feet. One of the troopers spotted a pendant among these treasures and his eyes widened in surprise as he picked it up.

'This was my sister's. Bandits attacked her village two months ago and she and her husband were killed.' The trooper turned angrily towards the bandit leader, shouting in Spanish as he held up the pendant. Hernandez pleaded and wept but the trooper fired and kept firing until he had emptied his pistol into his sister's killer. Sam glanced briefly at the crumpled body and then looked up in time to see the remaining bandit reach for a weapon. He fired as the Mexican raised his pistol and his adversary collapsed, clutching his chest. Then he led his companions back through the opening to rejoin the column.

Their return was greeted with relief and gratitude but then a tense silence descended as they resumed their journey, watched angrily by the disarmed bandits from the other side of the canyon. One of them shouted that he was Chico Hernandez and swore vengeance for the death of his brother and so many of his companions. Finally, they reached a point where they could see miles ahead to where the desert bordered the north-east corner of the State of Durango. Sam peered through his telescope and spotted a cavalry column accompanying three wagons. Far beyond it were the trees and rivers beneath the slopes of Durango's blue-topped mountains.

He passed the instrument to Boyd who gave a grunt of satisfaction. 'It's them all right. Let's just hope we can catch up.'

'We will. Fontaine's not getting away from me, even if I have to follow him into hell.' Sam's mouth was set in a determined line as he snapped the telescope shut that Boyd passed back to him. It was an expression the sergeant had seen many times before when Sam was in pursuit of an enemy and it usually ended in someone's capture or death. Boyd prayed that it would be Fontaine's rather than their own.

They made camp at sunset after descending some way towards the plain and passed an uneventful night before rising at dawn to continue their journey. They were in the desert once more, heading towards a village where Mendoza said they could get fresh water and supplies. After that they would climb up into the foothills, passing through a forest trail beneath the slopes of the mountains to overtake Dupin and his men. It took several hours to reach the village but the sight which greeted them on their arrival was sickeningly familiar: burned out homes, bloodstained corpses and the smell of decay. Buzzards were settling on the dead bodies and starting to peck the flesh from the bones so Mendoza organized some of his men into a burial party.

Dupin's troops had taken whatever food there was and thrown a corpse down the well so there was no fresh water available. Sam shook his head slowly as he looked at the carnage surrounding them.

'How can anyone resort to this?' he asked Mendoza.

The Mexican paused before giving his response. 'The people of this village were Juaristas. For a man like Dupin, that is enough.'

'You don't seem surprised, Captain.'

'Sadly, I am no longer surprised by such things because this is a sight I have looked upon many times before. All I can say is that when we catch up with Dupin and his men, they will pay dearly, very dearly indeed.' Mendoza tightened his grip on the reins of

71

his horse and swallowed hard. He may not have been surprised by what he saw but he still struggled to keep his emotions under control.

Sam noticed that a few of the bodies were those of soldiers in the red dolmans of the contra-guerrillas. It was clear that the villagers had made a vain attempt to fight back with their machetes but, outnumbered by men on horseback who were armed with guns, they never stood a chance. Then he noticed something else; a house that had been left intact. Puzzled, he called Boyd over and they approached the building cautiously. There was an Appaloosa tethered in a shelter at the side with a trough of water and some hay. They dismounted slowly and crept over to the door, opening it softly.

There was a bed in the far corner of the room and the man lying on it reached for the gun he had under the bedclothes. There was a loud click as Sam cocked his weapon.

'You'll be dead before you pull the trigger,' he warned.

The man slowly raised his hands and, stepping closer, Sam recognized him as Slade. Boyd pulled the bedclothes aside and they saw that the ex-confederate's leg was bandaged heavily.

'I had an unfortunate encounter with a machete,' explained Slade.

'You're going to have another one in a minute,' Boyd told him. 'However, this time you won't be so lucky because I've got a length of rope with your name on it and there's a tree out there that'll just do fine.'

Slade swallowed but said nothing. His pale blue eyes settled on Sam, hoping for a different response. Sam let him sweat for a moment before he spoke.

'No, let's take him with us. He might be useful.'

'But he can't ride. His friends left him here with food and water so he could catch them up in a couple of days. Slade's only gonna slow us down.'

'I think that if it's a choice between keeping up with us or hanging, Slade here will find that he's had a miraculous recovery. Isn't that right, Slade?'

The injured man nodded eagerly. 'Sure, I can keep up. The leg's getting better and I was going to ride out of here tomorrow anyway.'

Boyd shook his head vigorously. 'I've never questioned your orders before, sir, but I really don't see why we shouldn't just treat him like the murderer he is.'

Sam smiled in response. 'Dupin and Fontaine value this man and will want him back. Threatening to kill him might give us some leverage when we catch up with them, if it's needed.'

Boyd nodded slowly. 'I guess we can always hang him later, especially if we have any trouble.'

They hauled Slade to his feet and put him on his horse with his hands bound in front of him. Some of the troopers wanted to kill him but Mendoza saw the sense in Sam's plan and agreed to go along with it, though he would infinitely have preferred an execution. Boyd was deputed to ride behind the prisoner and keep a close eye on him, a task he appeared to relish. For his part, Slade showed no signs of being intimidated by his predicament, especially when he saw Consuela.

'It surely is a pleasure to see you again, Miss Martinez! Forgive my rudeness in not removing my hat but as you can see, my hands are tied at present.'

'I can assure you that it is only the removal of your head that would give me pleasure,' she responded coldly.

Slade laughed. 'I always did like a woman with spirit.'

Soon they turned west and began their climb into the Sierra Madre Occidental, their path through the steep, winding canyons one that was well known to Mendoza.

'I see you gentlemen have found a shortcut,' said Slade with apparent nonchalance.

'This brings us closer to the valley where Victoria de Durango is,' Boyd told him with evident satisfaction. 'That means we'll be in time to give your friends a surprise.'

Slade turned in the saddle and grinned back at his guard. 'That's assuming everyone arrives safely. These mountains can be very treacherous, you know.'

'Just remember I've got a gun aimed at you. Any sign of trouble and you'll be the first one over the edge, mark my words,' the sergeant replied.

The exchange left Sam feeling uneasy. If Slade somehow managed to give them the slip, he could get ahead, then double back across the desert and warn Dupin. He began to wonder if Boyd was right and they should have just hanged him after all. Dismissing such gloomy thoughts from his mind, he turned his attention to the trail in front of him.

The air cooled as they continued their ascent. Far below, the Nazas River rushed by to irrigate the desert plain. Slade peered over and looked at it thoughtfully. From this height it would be suicide but once they had dropped down a couple of hundred feet, the impact alone would not be enough to kill a man. Being a strong swimmer, he gave himself a reasonable chance of survival so it was just a question of biding his time. His leg still ached but was healing well and would be less stiff by tomorrow.

Behind him Boyd chuckled. 'Let me know if you feel like taking a dip. I'll be happy to send you on your way.'

'Why don't you give it a try, Yankee? I've been downwind of you long enough to know you could do with a bath.'

Boyd scowled but made no reply and Slade smiled to himself. Let the sergeant remain smug. All he had to do was stay patient and wait until it was time to make his move.

It was bitterly cold that night in the mountains and they huddled under their blankets in a cave spotted by Mendoza. Despite the good progress they had made, the men were dispirited by the lack of fresh supplies. Beans and biscuits were all that was left to eat and they were growing tired. Rising a little later the next morning, Mendoza ordered that they walk the horses for a stretch to allow them some rest. They mounted them again at noon, after reaching the peak of their climb and slowly began their descent.

Slade slowly loosened his bonds, fraying the rope against the pommel of his saddle. The horses quickened their pace as the path broadened and sloped downwards but he kept his mount close to the edge.

'We'll have overtaken your friends by now and there's nothing you can do about it,' Boyd told him.

Slade said nothing but kept his eye on their descent, judging the distance between him and the flowing rapids below. He fondled his horse's ears, a sturdy Appaloosa he had owned for several years. Ben would follow him anywhere and he was relying on that now. With a sudden movement, he leaped from the saddle and plunged headlong towards the teeming waters.

Boyd watched in amazement as his prisoner disappeared beneath the waves, quickly followed by his horse. He fired after Slade but it was no more than a reflex action. He had no chance of hitting him and Slade had little more chance of surviving. The whole column came to a halt and men peered over the side to see if the fugitive would come to the surface.

'I think I can see his horse,' said Consuela, pointing to a speck bobbing on the water.

Sam looked through his telescope and made out the Appaloosa swimming strongly across to the other side but there seemed to be no sign of Slade. 'That's definitely Slade's horse but I can't see him at all.' He scanned the waters eagerly but still saw nothing and now the horse was climbing up on to the river-bank.

'I guess he must have drowned,' said Boyd, 'and even if he didn't, he won't be able to get back across that desert on foot.'

'I guess not,' conceded Sam as he snapped the telescope shut.

Far below them, Slade hid among the foliage while Ben shook himself dry on the river-bank. He figured that his captors would try to find out whether he survived and had stayed under water, clinging to his mount's tail while he was pulled across. Once he felt sure that Mendoza's men were gone, he clambered out of the river and checked Ben over to ensure he had suffered no injuries. Then he swung himself into the saddle and headed off to warn Dupin.

Meanwhile, Sam and his companions continued their descent towards a clump of hills where Mendoza stopped to consult his map. Sam, Boyd and Milton gathered around and the captain pointed to a small village he had marked.

'In two days we will come out of these hills and reach San Miguel. It's a small place, nothing but a church, a cantina and a few peasants with their pigs so the French ignore it. They don't know that Juaristas come down from the hills to get food and fresh horses there. The villagers hide weapons for us, keep their eyes and ears open and tell us what our enemies are doing.'

'It sure sounds like a good place to stop, then,' commented Milton.

Mendoza pointed to another area on the map. 'There's another reason. Dupin will pass close by the village on his route to Victoria de Durango. We can launch a surprise attack from San Miguel and get those weapons back.'

'We're assuming that Slade is at the bottom of the Nazas River but what if he survived and warns Dupin in time?'

Mendoza shrugged. 'There's nothing we can do about that but such a thing does not seem possible. A man with a bad leg who jumps from such a height into a fast flowing river can expect only death.' The captain then folded his map and they continued their journey.

'I can't help thinking that Slade must have planned what he did, in which case he expected to survive. That could mean that he got away,' Sam remarked to Consuela later.

'But you saw his horse climb out of the river without him,' she said.

'That's true but there was no sign of a body floating downstream either. Now I come to think of it, that horse got out and stood on the river-bank. It didn't just run off.'

Consuela shrugged. 'So what? Horses are very

loyal and it waited for him. That doesn't mean Slade was still alive.'

'I guess not,' conceded Sam reluctantly. Perhaps it was best to just assume that the man was dead after all.

At that precise moment, Slade was riding briskly across the desert plain, his wet clothes drying quickly in the hot sun. Ben kept up a steady pace and after a few hours, a troop of red-coated cavalry accompanying three wagons emerged out of the haze. Slade stopped and waved as they drew nearer and Dupin rode ahead of his men to greet him.

'What are you doing out here, coming from that direction?' the colonel asked. He listened carefully to Slade's explanation and remained deep in thought for a moment until a smile spread across his features.

'Don't worry, Slade. I've got a little surprise of my own for Sam Curtis and his rebel friends; a surprise that will blow them all away completely!'

CHAPTER SIX

Sam soon forgot his worries about Slade. They had not gone much further when they heard the sound of horses in the valley below them. Mendoza called them to a halt and Sam passed him his telescope. Peering through it, he swore softly in Spanish.

'What is it?' Boyd asked anxiously.

'French cavalry, and they're heading this way.'

'Have they seen us?' said Milton.

Mendoza shook his head. 'That's unlikely but they know that there are rebels in these hills and they've come to look for them. Soon they will find us.'

'Not if we find them first,' Sam told him.

'A surprise attack, eh?' Mendoza rubbed his unshaven jaw thoughtfully. 'That's bold, *señor*. I like the way you think.' Then, raising his hand, he gave the order to charge. Soon they were galloping down the slope, firing at the enemy as they did so. The French barely had time to get themselves into a defensive formation and men dropped from their horses as they were hit by the rebel forces. By the time they were starting to fire back, Mendoza and his men were upon them, smashing into the cavalry's left flank so that they broke ranks almost immediately.

Sam fired into the scattering mass of Frenchmen while Milton slashed left and right with a sword. Boyd kept his horse's reins between his teeth while he fired a pistol with one hand and stabbed others at close quarters with a bayonet. It was hand to hand combat now, a desperate struggle for survival as the French cavalry recovered and regrouped in an effort to surround their assailants. Sam charged at two of the enemy as they moved in with swords to attack Boyd. He shot one man in the throat while Boyd dodged a blow from the second. Realizing he was out of bullets, he bent low in the saddle to scoop up a dead French officer's sword from the ground. The blade swung in an arc as he reached Boyd's second assailant, slicing through the Frenchman's jugular vein. The sergeant gave a brief nod of thanks before stabbing another attacker through the lungs with his bayonet.

Ahead of him, Sam saw once more the huge figure of Milton, still clearing a path through the enemy with his sword. Suddenly, he slumped forward, causing his horse to stumble as a bullet hit him in the chest. Dropping his weapon, Milton clutched at the wound and attempted a retreat but he was now encircled by enemies. Sam charged into them with a roar, shielding his comrade as he swung his blade about him. Enemy troopers fell to the left and right of him and then he seized the reins of Milton's horse to lead him from the field. A French lieutenant attempted to block his way but reeled under a blow from Sam's sword as the point scraped along his cheek. Blood spurted from a wound across the lieutenant's face and he barely managed to remain astride his horse.

There was a clearing a short distance away where Consuela was tending the wounded. She helped Sam lower Milton gently to the ground and then unbuttoned his clothing. The bullet had gone in at an angle, ripping downward through his chest and into his lungs. Milton's breath came in short gasps as blood seeped from the wound and pooled around his body.

'Thanks for what you did back there,' whispered the ex-confederate to Sam.

'You're a good soldier so it was the least I could do.'

Milton smiled wanly. 'You're not a bad soldier either – for a Yankee, I mean.' Then he coughed up blood in a sudden spasm, fell back and lay still.

'I'm sorry, Sam. You did your best to save him,' said Consuela consolingly.

'I'd best get back to the fighting.' He climbed wearily back into the saddle but saw that the French were now in headlong retreat, leaving the valley littered with their dead. Mendoza's men, however, had suffered relatively few casualties. Sam was glad when they got on their way again, away from the carnage of the battlefield, reflecting that victory after slaughter always left him with a hollow feeling rather than any sense of triumph.

Back in the desert, Fontaine was showing Slade the separate parts of a twelve-pounder mountain how-itzer. The short barrel and small carriage could easily be broken down and transported by wagon or pack animal. Sheridan had supplied a battery of four, care-fully hidden beneath the locomotive parts, and a supply of high-trajectory shells with fuses.

'Well, I have to take my hat off to that Yankee general. It's no wonder the south lost,' remarked Slade.

'Just wait until you see them assembled and in action,' Fontaine told him. 'These cannons are designed for attack when the enemy is behind some sort of fortification so they'll be particularly useful for what we have in mind.'

'What do you mean?'

'Well, the most obvious place for Curtis and the others to wait for us is a little village called San Miguel. I figure if we shell that place heavily enough, we'll destroy any defences supplied by the buildings and kill everything within range. Colonel Dupin thinks it's a wonderful idea.'

Slade nodded. 'I suppose you might call it poetic

justice. After all, Curtis was hoping to give us a little surprise, wasn't he?' Both men laughed.

Sam and his companions did not encounter any more patrols and the remainder of their journey was peaceful, though arduous. After two more nights out in the open, they at last reached San Miguel. A colonial style church with an ornately carved facade was the village's most interesting feature. There were two rows of whitewashed houses, some with thatched and others with clay tiled roofs. The place had once been a mission, hence the large church but the Franciscans had left over a hundred years ago and their friary had crumbled into ruins. The village which had grown up around it remained, however, and the people lined the streets to welcome the guerrillas, smiling and handing out flowers. A small group played guitars and the others joined in a folksong, which was gentle and pleasing to listen to.

'Tonight they will hold a *fiesta* for us,' announced Mendoza. 'All those who fight for Juarez are honoured guests when they come to San Miguel.'

Tables were quickly laid in the small square and the weary travellers were brought bowls of stew, tortillas, fruit and cheese. It was all washed down with cold beer and tequila while the musicians continued to play. Afterwards, Sam went down to the village stream where he bathed while one of the women washed his stained clothes, pounding them against the rocks at the water's edge. The entertainment carried on late into the night, with music, dancing and more liquor than Sam was used to. It was good to forget about fighting and getting the weapons back, at least for a while, but when morning came, he found that he had little memory of what had occurred the night before.

The sun's rays were like hot yellow fingers, stabbing him awake. Sam groaned as he sat upright on the hard narrow bed, still fully dressed apart from his boots, to find an entire family grinning at him. Looking around, he realized he was in one of the houses he had seen as he rode through earlier but had no recollection of when or how he had come to be there. Still, his hosts did not seem to mind and brought him a breakfast of maize and goat's milk. After eating, he shaved hurriedly and strode outside to find that the streets were largely deserted, apart from a few of Mendoza's men who had fallen into a stupor and remained sleeping outside all night.

By his reckoning, Sam and his companions were a day ahead of Dupin's men which meant that the enemy would probably be in the area that afternoon. He went to the stables to find his horse and fished the telescope out of his baggage, then climbed to the top of the bell tower to take a look. In the distance, a column was moving but it was too far away for him to make out the details. Nevertheless, who else could it be? Closing the instrument, he descended the steps and went in search of Mendoza. He was now sure that Dupin would be upon them well before sunset and it was time to make plans.

Fontaine was pleased by the swift progress they were making. The four howitzers had all been assembled and were being drawn behind them, ready for use as soon as they came to a halt within range of San Miguel. He knew that Mendoza had no artillery and could not hope to mount any effective defence against an attack of shells. If Curtis survived the battle, he would take great pleasure in hanging him afterwards. The thought brought a smile to Fontaine's lips and he spurred his horse to go a little faster. He had never before in his life so looked forward to combat.

Back at San Miguel, Mendoza cursed as the curtains in the upstairs bedroom of the cantina were drawn back to let in the daylight. The widow who owned the place sighed and buried her face in the pillow, snuggling her naked body closer to his.

'Come on, Captain. I told you I've seen them and now we must prepare.'

'What's the hurry? They won't be here for hours yet,' moaned Mendoza. 'Why can't you find yourself a woman and leave me in peace?'

'I'll be back in thirty minutes,' Sam said reluctantly. 'Just make sure you're ready.'

In the event, it was an hour before Mendoza actually got up and even longer before his hangover had abated sufficiently for him to consider planning an attack. Various strategies were explored, including a full-frontal assault and an approach from behind some foothills near the village to attack Dupin's left flank. Eventually, Sam pointed out that the troops would come within firing range of San Miguel itself, even if they decided not to stop there for the night. It was agreed that an attack from a fortified position would be the best option, especially since Dupin's men outnumbered them. The rest of the morning was spent fortifying gaps in the village walls before they settled down to wait.

Shortly after noon, Sam was on lookout when he saw the red-clad column approach. Curiously, it stopped suddenly some yards beyond rifle range. Then, with horror, he saw why as the battery of four twelve-pound howitzers were drawn into position at the front.

'They've got cannon – take cover!' cried Sam as he rang the church bell in alarm. He hurried down from the tower as the first shell whistled overhead. It landed on a thatched roof and then exploded into flames. Villagers dropped their belongings as they ran for cover, screaming in terror. More shells landed in quick succession, one of them hitting the friary ruins where several of Mendoza's men were resting before the battle. Three were killed immediately but a fourth staggered away, his clothes torn and burnt while blood ran from a wound on his head. A woman ran to his aid but was struck down by a large piece of shrapnel from yet another exploding shell.

Sam and Boyd herded people into the church as it was the only building both large enough to shelter everyone and strong enough to withstand the assault. Once they were all inside, the wounded could be tended in relative safety and the children comforted by their parents. Meanwhile, more shells pounded the village, their mournful shrieks culminating in a series of deafening explosions.

'We've got to find some way of knocking out those cannons,' Sam told Mendoza.

'Are you crazy, *gringo*? You'd get blown to the moon before you got more than ten yards outside.'

'A few of us could go around the side of them and head towards those foothills. They might not notice or just mistake us for villagers trying to make a run for it.'

Mendoza thought for a moment and then called over one of the older villagers. The two of them exchanged a brief conversation in Spanish and then the captain turned back to Sam. 'Some Juaristas hid weapons here, mainly rifles but they also left a barrel of gunpowder buried under a stable at the end of the street.'

'Well, what are we waiting for? Get two of your men and I'll come with Boyd.'

'We'd better put some ponchos and sombreros on before we leave,' suggested Boyd and they quickly donned these disguises.

Mendoza then called over two of his men and they made their way out into the deserted street. More shells exploded around them as they scurried past a row of houses until they reached the stable, which, thankfully, was still intact. Hurriedly, they pulled up some loose floorboards and lifted out the small barrel before loading it on to a mule. Then, mounting mules themselves, they trotted out through the back entrance and left the village. The animals brayed in terror as the bombardment continued and it took some effort to keep urging them forward. Soon, however, they reached the shelter of the hills.

Fontaine peered through his telescope at the five men making their escape. 'What do you make of that?' he asked, passing the instrument to Slade.

'It's just a few peasants trying to get away. Why bother with them?'

'You're right. A few more rounds and we'll be ready to enter San Miguel. Let's hope Curtis is still alive so we can watch him hang.'

At that moment, Dupin approached them. 'I've just had a message about Juaristas gathering about twenty miles north of here. I'm taking half the men to head back that way and launch an attack.'

'What about San Miguel?' asked Fontaine.

'I'm leaving you in command so finish up here and take the weapons on to Victoria de Durango like I ordered. The French will provide you with an escort from there to Mexico City. Then Slade here will return to the border area with the rest of my men but you're welcome to join up with us permanently if you want.'

'Maximilian's gold will suit me just fine, Colonel, so I'll say *adios*.'

'As you wish.' The two men exchanged salutes and then shook hands before Dupin led half the column away.

Up above them, Sam and his companions watched what was happening with interest. The colonel clearly thought that the bombardment must have killed off many of Mendoza's men. Otherwise he would not have decided to split his force.

'Let's wait a few minutes until he's out of sight,' suggested Mendoza. 'If Dupin hears the explosion he'll just assume it's his own cannons firing.'

Boyd balanced the barrel on the edge of a slope while he cut a length of rope to act as a fuse. Gouging out a small hole in the lid with his knife, he stuffed one end of the rope inside the barrel and got ready to light the other. They waited tensely while Dupin and his men disappeared in a cloud of dust. Then Boyd struck a match, lit the rope and gave the barrel a hearty shove to send it rolling down the hill towards the row of cannons below them.

The barrel quickly gathered speed and hit the target just before the fuse burned down. A trooper turned to move it away but it was too late and the barrel exploded a split second later, obliterating the first cannon and setting off further explosions which destroyed the others. Soldiers were flung up into the air and horses reared amid the fire and plumes of smoke. When it cleared, over twenty men lay dead upon the ground. Fontaine had been thrown by the blast but was otherwise unhurt. He staggered to his feet and looked around with horror at the carnage. Then he noticed the mangled, bloodied corpse of his friend Slade and let out a howl of rage.

Slade's faithful horse, Ben, had survived unhurt and Fontaine swung himself into the saddle in time to spot Sam and his companions heading back towards the village, their disguises now cast aside. The ex-confederate now took command, shouting orders at the remainder of his force, a group of confused, frightened men who were clearly in need of his decisive style of leadership.

'Come on, don't be afraid. The enemy had one tub of gunpowder and a lot of luck but there can't be many of them left. The streets will run with their blood before sundown, I promise you!' Fontaine waved his sword as he gave the order to attack and led the remnants of his cavalry troop ahead of the bedraggled infantry towards San Miguel.

Sam and his companions had now reached the church and Mendoza ordered his men to take up positions in front of the windows and in the bell tower. The priest, an elderly grey-bearded man in a worn cassock, protested that this was sacrilege.

'Where else should the people of San Miguel find

91

protection but in God's house?' Mendoza answered him and continued giving his orders. After all, it was the best defensive position they had and would keep the people safe.

Moments later, Fontaine entered the village at the head of his troops and looked around in puzzlement. There was no sign of Mendoza or his men apart from damaged buildings and some dead bodies. He scanned the rooftops anxiously but could see no-one. Then, he pointed at the bell tower as he spotted movement but before he could speak a hail of bullets was fired from inside the church.

'Take cover!' shouted Fontaine as his men scattered to hide among the surrounding buildings while he himself dived behind the well in the village square. He peered over the rim and cursed as he counted another six men dead. The church appeared impregnable and he had no equipment with which to lay siege to it. Looking around, he spotted a jug of oil lying on its side. Some of the contents had seeped out but there was still more than half left. Then he looked thoughtfully at the great wooden doors at the front of the church.

Fontaine fumbled in his pocket for a handkerchief, dipped one end in the oil, which he topped up with some brandy from his hip flask, and left the other trailing over the rim of the jug. He then lit the cloth before throwing the combustible mixture at the church door. The jug shattered and burst into flames which spread rapidly as the oil and brandy ran down the wooden planks. The door splintered as fresh tongues of fire leaped up and smoke billowed from the entrance.

Inside the church, Sam helped Mendoza's men to tackle the blaze by beating the flames with altar cloths soaked in water. Finally, the charred remains of the door collapsed on to the church steps, leaving a gaping hole. There were shouts from outside as Fontaine and his men charged the entrance while Sam and his companions took up defensive positions. The women and children crowded fearfully around the altar, apart from Consuela who had armed herself with a rifle.

A couple of Mendoza's men managed to drag a wooden pew across the doorway and the first soldiers to appear were shot down as they tried to get over the barrier. Those behind them remained outside firing rapidly into the church. A soldier to Sam's left was hit in the throat and fell back, gurgling as blood gushed from the wound. Another lurched forward as he stood up to get a clearer shot at one of Fontaine's men. Sam turned him over and saw that a gaping wound had appeared on the man's chest. The rebels returned fire and two more enemy soldiers were hit, their bodies tumbling down the church steps.

Suddenly, there were shots raining down on them from above. Fontaine had sent a few of his men climbing up the outside of the building to fire on them through the windows. This time Mendoza was hit, and fell back dead, a small round hole in the centre of his forehead. Sam picked up the dead man's revolving rifle and fired rapidly at the window directly above them. A trooper tumbled from the ledge with a choked cry, his body landing on the altar steps. Meanwhile, Consuela shot two other assailants who also fell to their deaths.

There followed a lull in the firing and an ominous silence. Then Sam heard the sound of galloping hoofs. Fontaine and his men were making a run for it and there was not a moment to lose!

CHAPTER SEVEN

Sam acted decisively. 'Get outside!' he shouted, running for the doorway with Boyd and the rebels at his heels. He emerged into the sunshine as one of the wagons was driven past and fired rapidly with the revolving rifle. The driver and the man next to him died in a hail of bullets while the wagon lurched into the side of a house and partly overturned. A second wagon followed close behind and the driver was forced to slow down to avoid crashing into the obstruction. Boyd had just enough time to leap on to the back, shoot the driver and his companion with a pistol and then grab the reins, drawing the precious cargo to a halt.

The third wagon, meanwhile, was disappearing in a cloud of dust and Sam resolved to get it back. It was then that he noticed Ben, the Appaloosa that had once belonged to Slade, tethered near the well. He leaped into the saddle and tore off down the street in pursuit of his quarry. Soon he was gaining on the wagon. A burly corporal was perched on the back, firing at him and a bullet whizzed past his ear. Sam fired back and the man tumbled to the ground. The driver had no-one else riding shotgun and, as he drew level with him, Sam saw that it was Fontaine. He raised his pistol to fire, just as the ex-confederate lashed him with the horsewhip and he fell back as the gun was struck from his hand.

Sam was now level with the back of the wagon and leaped on to it from his horse. There was a jolt as he landed and he slipped back, his feet dangling above the ground as he scrambled for a hold. He pulled himself up and crept along the top of the load. Fontaine sensed the movement behind and half turned as Sam jumped at him, the two men wrestling for control of the reins. Fontaine grabbed the whip again and raised it to strike but Sam grabbed his opponent's wrist, banging it against the edge of the seat so that he was forced to drop his weapon. Fontaine then lashed out with his fist and Sam was flung back to the other side of the wagon. As he struggled to sit upright, a boot was clamped against the side of his face, pushing him back until he was dangling precariously above the ground at high speed. Grabbing the foot with both hands, he twisted as hard as he could and Fontaine pulled his leg back with a yelp of pain.

Sam pressed home his advantage, seizing Fontaine's throat with both hands. He pressed down hard with his thumbs against his adversary's Adam's apple. Fontaine's face flushed purple, his eyes bulging in their sockets as he fought desperately to loosen Sam's grip. Then the wagon lurched sideways as the unguided horses went off the road and galloped down a ravine. Sam was lifted into the air and heard a crash as the wagon hit a tree before his head struck the ground and everything dissolved into an eddying pool of blackness.

When he came to, he was lying on the same bed he had slept in the night before. For a moment, he thought the whole thing had been a dream but he realized he was mistaken as soon as he tried to lift his head from the pillow. It was as if a team of blacksmiths had taken up residence inside his skull, banging hammers on anvils every second. Sam groaned and Consuela gently pushed him back against the pillow.

'You must rest,' she whispered gently.

'Did we get that wagon back?'

'It's quite damaged but not beyond repair.'

'Fontaine . . . what happened to him?'

Consuela shook her head. 'He must have got away, Sam. There were only three horses hitched to that wagon when we caught up with you and no sign of him anywhere.'

'We have to get out of here. Fontaine will fetch troops from Victoria de Durango to get those weapons back.'

'We'll be gone by then,' she said soothingly. 'The wagons will be fixed tomorrow and we can get on our way then.' Consuela placed a cold compress against his forehead and he fell once more into a restful sleep.

Sam still had a headache the next morning but felt well enough to travel. Besides, with Fontaine at large and on his way to warn the French garrison, he was anxious to get moving.

'I guess that cover story about the locomotive parts is no good now,' Boyd told him.

'You're right. The French will be looking out for that but the question is, what do we do instead?'

At that moment, a stench assailed his nostrils and he turned as a cart loaded with manure trundled past. The answer came to him with sudden clarity.

'Sergeant, get as much of that stuff as you can find. Cover the wagons and put the manure on top. Then tell all the men to disguise themselves as farmers.'

Boyd saluted smartly and hurried off to obey his orders. The villagers were happy to sacrifice both their fertilizer and some of their clothing in the service of the Juarista cause and Sam was more than happy with the result. He was confident that no one would consider searching for weapons under the loads they were now carrying and there was a good chance of reaching Tacambaro safely.

They turned back towards the Sierra Madre Occidental, climbing up from the foothills as they left the village. From there they would travel through the mountains, joining the Sierra Madre del Sur as they approached the State of Michoacan and finally reaching Tacambaro in about ten days' time. Hopefully, they would avoid enemy troops and might even come into contact with some more rebels.

Meanwhile, Fontaine had ridden all night and reached Victoria de Durango that same morning. Lieutenant Moreau listened to his story with interest while he stroked the scar that ran down the left side of his face.

'There are two of these Americans, you say?'

'Yes, Sam Curtis and Ben Boyd. Quite a few of the rebels are dead, including Mendoza.'

'I see. How many are left?'

Fontaine shrugged. 'Not more than ten, I shouldn't think.'

Moreau spread a map over his desk and traced a line from San Miguel to Tacambaro. 'If they've any sense, they won't wait around for us to turn up. You see where these mountain ranges join up? That is the route they'll take.'

'How long will it take to catch up?'

Moreau smiled ruefully. 'Rebels have crawled over every inch of those mountains; and it's a big area to search.'

'They're carrying a lot of weapons, Lieutenant. Catching them could make a big difference to the war, not to mention your career.'

'That thought had occurred to me. Besides, I have fought this Curtis you speak of; I'm sure he is the one who gave me this scar.'

'Then, like me, you have a score to settle.'

Moreau folded his map decisively. 'I suggest you get some rest. We leave at noon.'

Sam and his companions ascended the wooded slopes of the Sierra Madre Occidental and finally reached a vast canyon, beyond which more mountains stretched into the distance. They stopped and gazed upon the view for a few moments before continuing their journey.

'A man could get lost up here,' commented Boyd.

'I know the way. I travelled here with my father when he first made contact with the rebels,' Consuela told him.

'Do you know where we can find some of these rebels?' Sam asked.

She shook her head. 'No one knows the exact locations of their strongholds. When I came with my father, we met them at a point further south where we were blindfolded and taken to their camp. You don't find rebels out here; they find you.'

'Well, let's hope it's the rebels who find us and not the French,' replied Sam as he urged his mount forward.

It took them much of the day to cross the canyon, sometimes dismounting to walk the horses, but they saw no sign of anyone else although Sam sometimes had an uneasy sensation of being watched, which he dismissed from his mind. They made camp at sunset by a stream beneath a shelter of overhanging rock and passed an uneventful night before continuing their journey. They dropped down out of the canyon and climbed into the foothills of the next mountain range, eventually reaching a pine forest.

It was then that they saw a column of French cavalry approaching them out of the trees. The lieutenant leading them wrinkled his nose in disgust at the cargo of manure. Sam and Boyd kept their heads down and rode at the back while the officer interrogated the Mexican rebels, disguised as peasants, who accompanied the wagons. They all watched nervously as the lieutenant rode past them, staring intently at each man. At last, he drew alongside Sam and stopped. Then, in one swift movement he knocked the sombrero from Sam's head.

'I believe we have met before, Captain Curtis,' he said, fingering the scar which ran down his left cheek.

'I don't know what you're talking about. I'm just an American traveller hitching a ride with these farmers.'

The lieutenant smiled and called behind him. Fontaine now rode up from the back of the column and drew alongside the Frenchman.

'Lieutenant Moreau, allow me to introduce Captain Curtis and Sergeant Boyd.' Fontaine continued as the French troops gathered around to surround them: 'I'd like to compliment you on your disguise, Curtis. If you'd been smart enough to kill me, you might have got away with it.'

101

'I haven't finished yet,' Sam told him.

Fontaine laughed. 'Oh you have this time. I can guarantee that.'

'The weapons are underneath all that manure, I suppose,' said Moreau, clutching a handkerchief over his nose. He ordered some of the rebels to dismount and start unloading it which they did with some reluctance.

Fontaine pointed at Sam and Boyd. 'All right, you two. Get down and start shovelling.' When they hesitated he drew his revolver. 'I mean now,' he added.

It took some time to clear the dirt and shovel it over the side and Moreau then conducted a quick inspection of the weapons. He chattered excitedly to Fontaine in French, clearly delighted with what he had found. He then gave more orders to his men and the remainder of Mendoza's men were marched to a clearing a short way ahead by six men armed with rifles. Moments later, a volley of shots rang out while Sam and Boyd stood by helplessly. Consuela buried her face in her hands and wept.

'Don't upset yourself, Miss Martinez, they were just peasants,' Fontaine told her.

The slap she gave him turned his cheek red and the ex-colonel's eyes briefly flashed in anger but then he laughed again. 'I like a lady with spirit. I'll enjoy taming you.'

'Why are we still alive?' Sam asked the lieutenant when he returned.

'Emperor Maximilian has ordered that rebels are

to be executed but since you are both foreigners I want to seek further instructions regarding your fate. You will both be taken to Victoria de Durango and held there for the time being.'

'Couldn't you at least let the girl go?' pleaded Sam.

Moreau shook his head. 'Regrettably, no. She is a traitor and I have my orders to follow. The young lady must come with us.'

As they were led away with their hands bound in front of them, Fontaine rode cheerfully alongside. 'It's a pity Moreau's such a stickler for following orders,' he told Sam. 'I was looking forward to lynching you myself.'

'You didn't make such a good job of getting rid of us last time,' Boyd reminded him.

'Don't worry, Sergeant. If I'm ever given the chance to put a rope around both your necks, I'll make damn sure there's no chance of escape, even if it means standing around until the crows have pecked your eyes out.'

'Has it occurred to you that the Mexican government might not want to risk offending the United States? We might both be pardoned and released,' said Sam.

'Well, you'd better be ready to spend the rest of your life looking over your shoulder, Curtis. I'll come looking for you, I promise.'

Sam said nothing in reply and their journey continued in gloomy silence, broken only by Fontaine's whistling of various confederate songs. They descended towards the plain and prepared to make camp for the night at sunset. They would reach Victoria de Durango the following day, Sam now held out little hope of their being rescued.

He passed an uncomfortable night but was dozing shortly before dawn when he was awoken by shouting and the sound of gunfire. His hands and feet bound, Sam struggled to sit upright against the shelter of an overhanging rock. He looked about him and saw that the French were under attack from rebel forces. Though disciplined and well trained, Moreau's men barely had time to rouse themselves from sleep before the enemy was upon them and they were no match for their guerrilla tactics. The sentries lay with their throats cut so no alarm had been raised. Men were cut down as they reached for their guns, shot or slashed with machetes. When a dying trooper dropped a cavalry sword at his feet, Sam reached for it and hurriedly cut himself free. Now he too could join the fight.

At that moment he spotted Fontaine emerging from his tent, also armed with a sword. Sam ran at him and the southerner skilfully parried his first blow before moving in with a thrust of his own. Steel clashed upon steel as Sam forced him back and then slashed at his throat. Fontaine leaped nimbly to one side and the blade sang through thin air. The ex-confederate then lunged again and Sam narrowly avoided a wound to his side. A second blow was aimed at his head, which he quickly ducked, but then he lost his footing and fell backwards on to the ground. Fontaine thrust the point of his sword at Sam's chest and he rolled away just in time, leaping to his feet as the southerner pulled his sword out of the ground with a curse. Now Sam was on the attack again and his opponent retreated as he parried a series of blows.

The battle raged around the two combatants as they continued to thrust and stab at each other, neither man gaining the upper hand for long. Finally, Fontaine slipped on a pool of blood and lowered his guard. In an instant, Sam's blade was at his throat.

'Drop your weapon, Fontaine.'

His adversary obeyed with obvious reluctance. 'What are you waiting for? Why don't you just kill me?'

'I'm taking you prisoner so that when this is over I can return you to General Sheridan for your hanging.'

The French were now in disarray and those who could do so fled the field. A trooper on horseback almost mowed them down in his eagerness to get away and Sam was forced to jump back as the man rode past. In that instant, Fontaine vanished, disappearing into the melee. Sam made to run after him but his way was blocked by a group of rebels and he was forced to explain that he was on their side, allowing Fontaine time to make good his escape.

Sam was now confronted by a stout, middle-aged man who was smartly dressed in a colonel's uniform. He stroked a neatly trimmed beard, heavily salted with grey, as he looked him up and down.

'Forgive my curiosity, *señor,* but it is not usual to see a gringo dressed as a poor farmer. I noticed you fighting the enemy but what are you doing here?'

Sam introduced himself and gave an account of his, Boyd and Consuela's adventures since arriving in Mexico. The colonel did not interrupt but listened thoughtfully.

'I see. I am Colonel Eduardo Alvarez of the Republican Army of Mexico. I will now take responsibility for these weapons and deliver them safely to my comrades at Tacambaro.'

'Thank you, Colonel, but I must insist on coming with you.'

Alvarez raised his eyebrows in surprise. 'I assure you that it is not necessary, Captain. You have already had quite an ordeal and this is not your fight, after all.'

'I appreciate your concern but my orders were to deliver the weapons myself and I intend to stay with them until that mission is accomplished.'

Alvarez smiled. 'I understand, Captain. You speak as a true soldier, whereas I was a lawyer before the French intervention in my country. You are most welcome to join us.'

'I hope that includes me too, Colonel.'

Both men turned as Consuela approached and

Sam was relieved to see that she was unhurt. Alvarez exchanged a brief conversation with her in Spanish which Consuela then explained to Sam.

'The colonel was just telling me that he knew my father when they were both practicing law.'

'I am sorry to hear of his death; he was a fine man,' added Alvarez sombrely.

At that moment a junior officer approached, saluted smartly and informed the colonel that the prisoners were assembled although Moreau and two of his men had managed to escape. Alvarez immediately gave orders that those captured were to be shot. Sam understood enough Spanish to know what had transpired and immediately began to protest.

'I beg you to reconsider, sir. How can your cause be defended honourably when captured men are murdered in cold blood?'

'My scout saw what Moreau and his men did to their prisoners yesterday and so did you. A similar fate befell my own son. The only way to drive the French out of Mexico is to be as ruthless in battle as they are. I may not be a career soldier like you, Captain, but that much I have learned.'

Sam saw that it was useless to argue and could only listen in horror as the shots rang out. Nevertheless, the rebels were being treated brutally by a foreign army on their own soil and it was difficult to have much sympathy for the French after having witnessed the previous day's massacre.

After a rest, a wash and some breakfast, they were

107

ready to leave the carnage of the battlefield and head back towards the relative safety of the Sierra Madre Occidental. Fontaine's escape played on Sam's mind as he rode alongside the rebel column with Boyd and Consuela but they urged him to forget about it.

'What can he do?' Boyd asked. 'Fontaine left Victoria de Durango with troops who were all slaughtered. When he returns as the only survivor, no officer will risk sending more men after those weapons.'

'Ben's right,' Consuela told him. 'Fontaine may be a wicked man with a lot of luck but there's not much he can do now.'

'I guess so,' conceded Sam reluctantly. 'I just don't like the idea of him getting away.'

As their journey progressed, Sam forgot his worries about Fontaine and turned his attention to ensuring that the wagons passed safely along the narrow pass that wound through the mountain range ahead of them. It was a slow, arduous journey and by the time their path broadened out once more into a series of wooded slopes, they were all exhausted. After sleeping heavily that night, they continued once more at dawn, their limbs still aching.

CHAPTER EIGHT

Fontaine and Moreau were shrouded in gloom as they trekked wearily back to Victoria de Durango. The two troopers following behind said nothing as the officers cursed the bad luck which had assailed them.

'I would have been promoted to captain were it not for those damned rebels. Now I could face a court martial for reckless conduct.'

'It wasn't reckless, Moreau. We recaptured the weapons but no-one could have predicted that attack.'

The lieutenant shrugged in response. 'What does it matter now? We've no chance of getting those weapons back anyway. The Juaristas at Tacambaro will hold on to their position less than a hundred miles from the capital.'

Fontaine was silent for a moment before he asked his companion a question. 'Tell me, how badly are those weapons needed?'

'Our troops are quite well equipped although we could use them, of course.'

'I see. The most important thing, then, is to stop the Juaristas getting their hands on them. Is that correct?'

'Yes, I suppose so. What are you getting at?'

'I was thinking about what happened when Colonel Dupin lost his cannons. They were just blown up by the enemy. Curtis could have stolen them but he didn't need to.'

'Do you think we could play the same trick on him?'

'I don't see why not. A small team of men armed with gunpowder and fuses could use the cover of the mountains to launch that kind of attack.'

'That's true,' conceded Moreau, 'but there are lots of rebels in those mountains. We would be taking a great risk.'

'We would but isn't that the nature of soldiering? If you want glory, Moreau, it has to be earned.'

'What's in it for you?'

'I've had my fill of glory. Now I just want gold. Emperor Maximilian will pay handsomely to prevent those weapons from falling into the wrong hands.'

'When we reach Victoria de Durango you can ask him that yourself. He's making an official visit to inspect the troops.'

Fontaine smiled for the first time since their defeat. 'When I see His Majesty I'll name my price.'

*

Meanwhile, Colonel Alvarez was leading his men higher into the Sierra Madre Occidental. The air was cool and scented with pine from the surrounding forest with neither sight nor sound of another human being. Nevertheless, Juarista rebels were known to hide out in this area and the silence did not mean that no one was watching them. The woods stretched for miles ahead, bordered by a stream and there was abundant game to supplement their supplies of food.

'Does the landscape continue like this?' Sam asked the colonel.

'It does for another day or so. We will pass through more canyons and dry broadleaf forests when we reach the Sierra Madre del Sur. You'll be able to see the Pacific Ocean as we approach Michoacan.'

'Are there any dangers I should know about?'

'Not if we stick to our trail through the mountains. There are more French troops in Michoacan so there is a risk of attack when we reach the plain but we'll be on our guard.'

Sam nodded as he counted the number of men and weighed up their chances in the event of an attack.

'Don't worry, Captain. These weapons will reach Tacambaro safely. I'm certain of that much,' Alvarez assured him.

'I'm sure you're right,' responded Sam politely but he was not taking anything for granted. He exchanged glances with Boyd and saw the older man finger the butt of his revolver. Their recent experiences had taught him to be wary too.

Fontaine and his companions rode through Victoria de Durango's maze of narrow streets until they reached a colonnaded building, which served as the emperor's residence during his visit to the city. Moreau informed Maximilian's equerry that he had news of some military importance and he and Fontaine were quickly ushered into the monarch's presence.

His Imperial Majesty Emperor Maximilian of Mexico was a dapper fair-haired man with a crisply curling beard and the hooded eyes and aquiline nose of his Hapsburg forbears.

'I understand you have important news, gentlemen,' he said. His French was impeccable but the Austrian accent was unmistakeable.

Moreau explained how he and his men had captured the weapons bound for Tacambaro only to be overwhelmed by rebel forces. Maximilian listened attentively, his face grave, but seemed interested when the lieutenant described Fontaine's plan to destroy the weapons. He turned and looked with interest at the ex-confederate.

'I assume you have some experience in these matters?' he inquired in English.

'Yes, Your Majesty. I served with the confederacy and reached the rank of colonel.'

'A noble cause, I think. So, are you confident that this plan of yours will work?'

'Nothing is certain, sir, but I believe it is worth the attempt. I lost everything when the south was defeated so I'm used to taking risks.'

'Well, Colonel Fontaine, if you succeed in this endeavour, I will see to it that you are paid ten thousand American dollars in gold. There is also land available here should you decide to stay in Mexico.'

'Your Majesty is very generous,' replied Fontaine.

Maximilian turned back to Moreau. 'Take whatever you need from the stores and some fresh horses. I will give you my written authorization and clear this mission with your commanding officer.' The emperor drew a sheet of paper from his desk and wrote on it quickly before signing the document and affixing his seal. 'It is imperative that the rebels holding Tacambaro do not receive those weapons, so do whatever you can,' he added as he handed the note to Moreau.

They both bowed and backed out of the room quickly before heading off to collect what they needed. The two troopers who had survived the battle with Moreau followed behind and soon they were leaving the town behind them again as they set off in pursuit of the rebels.

The next two days passed uneventfully. Alvarez led the column through pine forests and across another broad canyon. They exchanged greetings with a small party of guerrilla fighters but otherwise saw and heard no-one. They then dropped down towards another wooded area and Consuela pointed to a lake a short distance away. They rode towards it to water the horses and refill their canteens and then Consuela announced that she was going for a swim.

'We're going to stop for a rest on in that clearing a mile further on. Rejoin us when you've finished,' Alvarez told her.

Consuela waited until the soldiers had disappeared from view and then stripped off before diving into the cool water. She swam underneath for a while before emerging in the centre of the lake, where she floated on her back, gazing at the cloudless sky above. Her thoughts turned to Sam Curtis, as they frequently did these days. However, he was preoccupied by the job he had to do and had so far shown no signs of any attraction towards her. Consuela sighed, longingly. If only he would give her some hint of returning her affections instead of being so correct in his behaviour at all times. She found herself wishing that he would just drop his reserve and kiss her impulsively. Any other man who tried such a thing would be slapped hard across the face but not Sam Curtis. No, she would respond with abandon. She allowed herself a few more minutes to imagine such a thing before swimming reluctantly back towards the lakeside.

Claude Dubois and Jacques Laval watched furtively as Consuela's naked form emerged from the lake, water running in rivulets down her fulsome breasts and broad hips before pooling at her feet.

'She looks magnificent,' whispered Dubois. 'Let's grab her right now.'

'All right,' agreed Laval, 'but it was me who spotted her so I get to go first. I haven't had a woman in months.'

Suddenly, both men sensed movement from behind and turned to see Fontaine standing over them.

'That woman is with the men carrying the weapons we're after, which means they can't be far away.'

'Does that mean we can't amuse ourselves with her?' asked Dubois.

'We'll see. If you manage to bring her along without drawing any unwelcome attention I might let you have your fun later. Right now I want her unharmed. Is that clear?'

The troopers both nodded their assent and crept forward as Consuela pulled on her clothes. She had her back to them and they made no sound at first. A twig snapped under Laval's boot as he reached her and she turned, her mouth opening in a scream but it was too late. A large hand was clamped over her lips, choking off any sound and an arm wrapped firmly around her waist, lifting her feet from the ground. Consuela struggled desperately but her captor was immensely strong. His companion was thin and wiry but adept in his movements and easily dodged her attempts to kick him as he approached to knock her out with the butt of his revolver. Her eyes widened in terror as she was clubbed across the forehead and then she slumped, unconscious against Laval's burly frame.

The two Frenchmen then slung Consuela across her horse's back, bound her hands and feet and made their way back towards Fontaine who grinned at them in satisfaction. Moreau, however, was alarmed when they returned to their makeshift camp.

'What are you doing bringing her along?' he asked Dubois and Laval angrily. 'We are not here on a merry jaunt and the girl will only slow us up!'

'They acted on my orders,' Fontaine told him. 'The girl is Consuela Martinez and she's travelling with Curtis, Boyd and the others, which means they can't be far away.'

'I don't understand. Won't kidnapping her put them on alert?'

Fontaine smiled. 'Yes and then Curtis will come after her himself, possibly with Boyd in tow. We'll ambush them and have three prisoners.'

Moreau shook his head. 'You won't be able to trade captives for those weapons.'

'I know that,' replied the ex-confederate and then explained what he was really planning to do.

Moreau's scepticism suddenly vanished. 'You have the mind of a genius. With men such as you, how was the South ever defeated?'

'I ask myself that question every day,' Fontaine told him.

*

Sam was getting worried. An hour had gone by and there was no sign of Consuela's return. What could be taking her so long? Meanwhile, Alvarez was anxious for them to get on their way again.

'I'll just head down to the lake and find out what's going on,' Sam said.

'Very well, Captain, but we must leave in ten minutes.'

Sam galloped down to the lake, calling Consuela's name as he approached but there was no response. He dismounted and examined the footprints near the water, noting three sets of them and signs that there had been some sort of disturbance or struggle. Then he noticed something else – a piece of cloth snagged on the branch of a tree. Could it have been torn from Consuela's blouse? He followed a set of hoof prints with two sets of footprints running beside them. Her horse had clearly been led away, presumably with her on it. Sam fought down a rising tide of panic, leaped back on to his horse and sped off back towards the column.

'She's been kidnapped, I'm certain of it,' he told Alvarez, explaining what he had seen.

The colonel rubbed his beard thoughtfully. 'She's probably been taken by bandits.'

'That's what I figured. I'll take Boyd and get after them. Then we'll rejoin you as soon as we can.'

'You can take a few of my men as well,' Alvarez said.

'Thanks for the offer but there were probably just

117

two of them and we need to travel fast if we're to catch up.'

He and Boyd followed the trail, which led away from the lake and then along a route which ran parallel to the one being taken by Alvarez and his men. It became clear that the two men who had taken Consuela were quickly joined by two more and Sam began to regret not having accepted the offer of reinforcements. At least the culprits had made no attempt to hide their trail, which suggested that they had no expectation of being followed. Sam hoped that the element of surprise would work in his and Boyd's favour.

Consuela was now awake and sitting up on her horse, her hands bound to the pommel of her saddle and her feet to the stirrups. Her head ached and she groaned with every jolt while trying to ignore the leering soldiers on either side of her.

'Don't worry, Mademoiselle. You'll soon feel better and then I'll show you a good time,' Laval told her.

'Yes, then it will be my turn,' added Dubois.

'That's enough. Keep your minds on fixing those weapons,' Fontaine told them and both men reluctantly moved forwards.

'You won't get far,' Consuela told him defiantly. 'Captain Curtis will be coming after you once he realizes what has happened.'

'Indeed, I hope for nothing less.' Then Fontaine leaned towards her and whispered, 'I have a special plan for both of you, so don't spoil it by trying to escape. Otherwise I'll be forced to hand you over to those two admirers of yours.'

Despite the warmth of the day, Consuela shivered. It seemed that she was in even worse trouble than she had first thought.

Sam and Boyd doggedly followed the trail left by their quarry until they spotted a group of four in the distance leading a female captive. They spurred their horses on to catch up but just as they began to close the gap, the men they were following disappeared from view. Finding themselves in a clearing sur-rounded by rocky outcrops, they stopped to look around. The trail had gone cold near a waterfall, which poured into a lake.

'Maybe they crossed to the other side,' suggested Boyd.

'No, we'd still see them ahead of us and anyway, the water would have slowed them down,' said Sam. He looked up at the surrounding rocks. 'They're here somewhere.'

Then a familiar voice rang out. 'There are four rifles trained on you. Put your hands up and don't try anything.'

'What have you done with Consuela, Fontaine?'

'Look up to your left, Curtis,' was the reply.

Sam looked up and saw Consuela, her feet near the edge of a precipice while behind her, rifle in hand, stood Fontaine.

'One false move and she goes over the edge!' the ex-confederate warned them. 'Now, take off your gun-belts and throw them away from you, followed by your rifles!'

They had no choice other than to obey. Then, a wiry French soldier appeared from behind a rock and approached them slowly, his rifle pointed straight ahead. Without taking his eyes off either man or allowing the barrel of his gun to waver, he bent down slowly and cast their weapons into the water. Then he stood up again, all the while keeping his rifle trained on his captives.

The others then emerged from their hiding places, each man armed and ready to shoot. Fontaine still held Consuela in front of him and Sam also recognized Lieutenant Moreau. There was also another Frenchman with a bull neck and a broad frame whom he did not recognize.

'Well done, Dubois,' Moreau told the wiry soldier before turning to his burly companion. 'Laval, tie them on to their mounts.'

Laval did as he was ordered and then he and Dubois went to fetch their own and the officers' horses, conveniently tethered in a nearby cave.

'You've got what you wanted, Fontaine. Now let the woman go.'

'You're very gallant, Captain, but I haven't quite finished with her yet.'

'What do you think you're going to achieve?' demanded Boyd. 'Those weapons are on the way to

Tacambaro and there's not a damn thing you can do about it. Killing us won't change that!'

'You'll find out what we can do soon enough, won't he, Lieutenant.'

Moreau smiled in response but said nothing. Sam and Boyd exchanged worried glances while their two enemies consulted a map and engaged in a hushed discussion. Meanwhile, the others returned with the horses and Consuela was once more lifted into the saddle. Sam winced as he noted the lascivious glances given to her by Dubois and Laval and he struggled impotently against his bonds.

'Don't worry, you'll be with her in eternity soon enough,' chuckled Moreau as he mounted his horse to take the lead, Fontaine following close behind. Sam had no idea where they were going but they continued along a path that ran roughly parallel to the route Alvarez was taking, passing through a range of foothills and wooded slopes.

'What the hell do you think they're planning?' Boyd asked Sam.

'They can't attack Alvarez with just four men so they must be meeting up with reinforcements. You saw them looking at that map. Presumably, they were checking out the way to their rendezvous.'

'That makes sense in one way, I guess, but why kidnap Miss Martinez and then us? I just don't get it.'

Sam shrugged. 'I don't either but we must fit into their plans somehow.'

Their captors ensured that they kept up a brisk

pace, even when they turned and climbed up on to higher ground. Then, as sunset approached, they reached the crumbled ruins of what appeared to have once been a Spanish fort, built at the time of the conquistadores but now long since abandoned. Fontaine called them to a halt as they assembled inside what remained of its walls.

'This is where you get to spend your last night on earth, gentlemen,' he told Sam and Boyd cheerfully.

'What about her?' asked Sam, nodding towards Consuela.

'I agree that she seems too pretty to die but I'm afraid it will be her last night as well.'

'For God's sake, man. Have you no pity?'

'Pity is a luxury for times of peace,' Fontaine told him. 'However, it will be a quick death. I can promise you that much.'

'Just what do you intend to do with us?' asked Boyd.

'I see no harm in ending the suspense,' remarked Moreau who now joined them.

'Very well, I'll tell you. We have some small sacks of gunpowder and fuses with us. It is a simple matter to tie them around your necks and send you bound and gagged on horseback towards the wagons when we catch up with Alvarez and his men tomorrow.'

'Your deaths will serve a very useful purpose,' added Moreau. 'We aim to destroy all three wagon-loads of weaponry and probably kill half the men guarding them.'

'The rest of them will come after you.' said Sam defiantly. 'Alvarez won't rest until he's put all four of you in the ground.

'Nice try,' laughed Fontaine 'but we'll be long gone by the time the survivors have recovered their wits.'

Their captors ignored them after that, apart from grudgingly providing a little food and some water. The three prisoners huddled together against what had once been the inner wall of the fort. They were all bound securely so escape seemed impossible and they lapsed into a morose silence as night fell. Fontaine, Moreau and Laval were all sound asleep while Dubois kept the first watch. It was then that Consuela whispered the details of a desperate plan to Sam and Boyd – one that might just work.

CHAPTER NINE

Consuela slowly shuffled towards Dubois, calling his name softly to attract his attention but without waking his companions. The Frenchman turned, looked around to check that he was unobserved and then crept towards her.

'If I am to die tomorrow, I want to experience a man's passion first. I've seen the way you look at me but that brute, Laval, does not appeal to me at all. What do you say?'

'I'm supposed to be on guard. If Lieutenant Moreau hears us I'll be in trouble.'

'Oh come. We won't make much noise and you'll be back on guard before anyone wakes up. Besides, you wouldn't refuse my last wish, would you?'

Their physical proximity and Consuela's coquettish tone inflamed the Frenchman's lust and suddenly, Dubois made up his mind. He helped her to her feet and tried to lead her away behind some ruins. She made as if to stumble and fell against him.

'It will be much easier if you untie me,' she whispered.

Dubois shook his head. 'I daren't do that.'

'But you're armed and much stronger than I am. You'll shoot me if I try to escape and you want us to have fun, don't you?'

Impulsively, Dubois cut her bonds and led her further away from the others, stopping behind the remains of a tower. He fell upon her at once, his hands pawing at her lithe body and Consuela forced a smile as she struggled to conceal her revulsion.

'Let me take my clothes off,' she urged him and he relaxed his grip as she pulled away. Slowly she began to unbutton the top of her blouse and Dubois stared at the cleavage between her breasts.

'Now, you must close your eyes before I go any further and don't open them until I say so,' she told him, waving an admonitory finger.

Dubois foolishly obeyed, his wits clouded by desire and Consuela swiftly removed the stiletto she concealed inside the top of her boot. The Frenchman sensed a movement and opened his eyes just as the blade was plunged directly into his heart. He gasped as she withdrew the weapon and then fell to the ground, dead.

Consuela quickly removed his gun-belt and took the rifle he had propped up against the wall. Then she crept back to her companions and untied them. Just as she finished doing so, they all froze at the sound of one of their captors stirring. A vast shape lumbered across from them in the moonlight as Laval made his way to the far wall to urinate. Putting his finger to his lips, Boyd took the stiletto from Consuela and approached the Frenchman stealthily from behind. Laval made barely a sound as the blade slid between his ribs and Boyd lowered his body gently to the ground. Then he removed the dead man's pistol before rejoining his companions.

Fontaine and Moreau remained fast asleep, oblivious to the danger they were in, while their former prisoners debated in whispers about what they should do with them.

'I say let's just kill 'em like they deserve,' said Boyd.

Sam shook his head. 'No, killing men in their sleep makes us just as bad as they are. I won't stoop to that.'

'We could just leave them here but take their horses and weapons,' suggested Consuela. 'That way we wouldn't have to kill them.'

Sam considered this for a moment. 'There's always the chance they'd run into some contra guerrillas or French troops. Besides, they know all about the weapons and where we're taking them. It's not worth the risk.'

Boyd sighed. 'Then I guess we'll just have to take them prisoner.'

Sam, Boyd and Consuela then approached the two men, their guns cocked and ready to fire at the least sign of resistance. Sam kicked the soles of Fontaine's feet, then jammed the muzzle of his revolver under the ex-confederate's chin. The southerner's eyes widened in terror but he did not make a sound as Sam reached behind to pick up his gun-belt. Moreau surreptitiously reached for a concealed weapon but grimaced as Boyd clamped a booted foot down heavily on his wrist.

'Just give me an excuse to shoot, Frenchie. It'll make my job a whole lot easier.'

Moreau wisely remained still while his gun was taken from him and he and Fontaine were then hauled to their feet. The two prisoners were bound together while Sam and Boyd took turns guarding them until dawn. As soon as it was light enough to travel, Sam ensured that Fontaine and Moreau were tied securely on to their horses before leading the party back to intercept Alvarez and his men.

The morning was warm and bright by the time they saw the column advancing across a canyon towards them. Alvarez slowed to a halt as he drew level with Sam and the others. He looked over their prisoners with surprise.

'So these are the mysterious bandits. They don't look very threatening now, do they, Captain? Still, we'll make sure they don't interfere with us again.'

Sam explained what Fontaine and Moreau had planned to do and the colonel shook his head in disgust.

'What kind of men are you that you can blow up a woman and these poor horses as well as your enemies?'

'Well, what can you expect?' asked Boyd. 'The French eat horses and southerners keep slaves so we know they ain't civilized.'

Alvarez laughed loudly. 'You are right, my friend. Let's go a little further on and I'll show you how to deal with such savages.'

They had not gone much further before they entered a wooded area and Alvarez soon found what he was looking for. He pointed to a tree with a long thick branch about half way up.

'That should take the weight of two men. Sling two lengths of rope around it,' he told one of his men who climbed up and did as he was told.

'I see that I'm to be hanged,' remarked Fontaine drily. 'I was hoping for something rather more imaginative, though not more painful, of course.'

'I assure you that you will not be disappointed,' Alvarez told him and then ordered their horses to be led under the branch. Both men were cut free from their bonds and told to raise their hands above their heads. Their wrists were then bound to the ropes hanging from the tree and their horses led away from under them.

'So, instead of shooting us like soldiers you're leaving us to die of exposure' remarked Moreau.

Alvarez shook his head. 'I intend nothing so prolonged, I assure you.' Then he ordered that the sacks of gunpowder and fuses be fetched from the prisoners' saddle-bags and placed underneath the men's feet. The colonel then lit a cigar and drew on it with a sigh of satisfaction before asking the condemned men if they had any last words.

'I'll see you in hell, Colonel,' Fontaine told him while Moreau whispered a prayer.

Alvarez dismounted and threw the prisoners' gun-belts down, just tantalizingly out of reach and lit both fuses before swinging agilely back into the saddle. The column was then urged forward to prevent them all from being blown sky high and they went on their way. Sam said nothing although he would rather have taken Fontaine back to Texas for trial. Nevertheless, the man would have hanged anyway and being blown up was more reliable if one hoped for a swift death.

As soon as the column had disappeared from view, Fontaine began to haul his body up until his chin was level with the branch above and then pushed his weight back down as forcefully as he could, urging Moreau to do the same while the fuse continued to burn down beneath them. 'Come on – it's our only chance!'

The Frenchman obeyed and the wood made a groaning sound as their movements weakened the branch. They pulled up and pushed down harder and faster in a series of frenzied movements while death inched closer all the while. At last, with seconds to spare, the branch snapped and they both rolled as they hit the ground before a deafening explosion rang out, turning the tree to a blackened

129

stump. The rebels heard the sound almost a mile away and would, no doubt, have been astonished to see both men stumble to their feet having suffered only a few cuts and bruises.

Their horses had been left tethered nearby and Fontaine, after quickly dusting himself down, went to fetch them. Searching among the saddle-bags to find what had been left he gave a sudden shout of glee.

'What is it?' asked Moreau.

'They missed some of the gunpowder,' the southerner replied, holding up two bags. 'There might just be enough left to do the job after all.'

Moreau shook his head in disbelief. 'Are you mad? We've just managed to escape with our lives and now you want to go after those weapons all over again!'

'This time we'll wait until the wagons are delivered, create an explosion in the town and ride off to Mexico City with the weapons. That's far better than just destroying them.'

'Just how are you going to do that? The place will be crawling with soldiers.'

Fontaine shrugged. 'I'll think of something. A disguise would be the best option.'

'Perhaps you could go in as a clown but then you wouldn't need a disguise for that,' said Moreau with disdain as he mounted his horse. 'I've had enough of your schemes, Fontaine. From now on you're on your own.'

Fontaine had put his gun-belt back on by this time and he spoke calmly as he met his companion's stare

130

with hard, grey eyes.

'If you try to run out on me, I'll kill you,' he told Moreau.

The Frenchman could see that the American was not bluffing and reached for his pistol but a bullet ripped through his lungs before he had even drawn his weapon; the second bullet penetrated his heart. Moreau was dead before his body hit the ground but Fontaine turned him over to make sure. He glanced down at his handiwork without remorse and then prepared to follow the column's trail to Tacambaro. Killing Moreau had been a necessity as far as he was concerned. The Frenchman might have talked if captured by other rebels while on his way back to Durango de Victoria. Then the local Juaristas would have been on the lookout for Fontaine himself. As things stood, those who mattered would continue to assume that Colonel Henry Lucius Fontaine was dead, which suited his purpose just fine.

'We should reach our destination in less than a week,' Alvarez told Sam. 'No doubt, you will be pleased to finally unload your cargo.'

'You're right, Colonel. I know that this is all in a good cause but those weapons haven't brought me any luck so far. In fact, they've been a damned pain in the ass.'

Alvarez laughed. 'Let's just hope they give even more trouble to the French and the royalist boot-lickers who keep Maximilian on his throne.'

Sam caught a sudden movement out of the corner of his eye as he glanced up at the canyon surrounding them, followed by the flash one sees when sunlight reflects off the barrel of a gun.

'There's someone up there, watching us.'

Alvarez shrugged in response. 'You're probably right. There are plenty of guerrilla fighters in these parts who would all willingly die for Juarez and our republic. It should please you to think that we are being watched over.'

Boyd grinned when he heard these words; 'It sounds like we've got ourselves some guardian angels, Captain,' he told Sam. 'At least, that's what my old Irish mother would say.'

High above them, Chico Hernandez lowered the telescope through which he had been watching the column below. He recognized the two *gringos* at once as the men who had helped to kill his brother and so many of his companions. Ever since he took over as leader of the remaining ten bandits, Chico had sworn daily to avenge the deaths of his brother and his friends. Now it seemed that he was going to get the chance and capture three wagonloads of goods into the bargain.

'Is it them, Chico?' asked Paolo, his impetuous younger brother.

Chico nodded silently in response.

'What are we waiting for? When do we attack?'

'You are brave, Paolo, but young and foolish. We will attack when our enemies do not expect it.'

Paolo accepted the rebuke and wisely said nothing. He knew that Chico was a more experienced fighter than he was and no doubt had good reasons for choosing to delay. Nevertheless, he was eager to fight and hoped that his brother would let him kill one of the *gringos* himself.

'How many uniforms did we take from those Juaristas we ambushed yesterday?' Chico asked his younger brother.

'We kept a dozen of them. The others were too badly damaged or did not fit any of our men.'

'There will still be enough for everyone. Go fetch them.'

Paolo hurried to do Chico's bidding and soon returned with the garments. The older man examined them carefully while his brother watched with interest.

'What are you planning to do?'

'We're going to play at soldiers, Paolo. We will greet these Juaristas as comrades and ride with them until it is time to strike.'

'When will that be?'

Chico smiled. 'Be patient, my brother. To overcome a more powerful enemy, you must first convince him that you are his friend.'

Alvarez had called a halt for the day when a group of men approached their camp, all in the uniform of the Republican Army of Mexico. Their leader introduced himself with a smart salute as Lieutenant Hernandez.

'We ran into some French troopers a few days ago and took some heavy losses. I spotted your column and thought it might be safer if we joined up with you.'

'I see. You were on patrol out here I take it?' replied Alvarez.

'Yes, sir. We've been out in these mountains for months, attacking royalist forces when we get the chance.'

Alvarez eyed the lieutenant and his men critically. They seemed slightly ill at ease and some of their uniforms did not fit too well. 'How many of you were there originally?'

Hernandez hesitated before giving his reply. 'Er . . . forty, sir.'

'Who was in command?'

'Captain Montez, sir. He was killed in the attack.'

'Well, you're too small in number to keep patrolling out here. We're on our way to Tacambaro. I'm sure the troops there could do with a few rein-forcements so fall your men in and get some rest.'

The lieutenant saluted again and Alvarez watched him march away. His men looked a surly bunch; rough and ill disciplined. Perhaps it was the time they had spent fighting a guerrilla war against the French, although his own troops had remained smart and well drilled. Sam also observed the way the new arrivals slouched, wore their caps pushed back on their heads and had tunic buttons undone.

'When they reach Tacambaro, they'll soon get knocked back into shape,' said Alvarez, as if reading

134

his thoughts.

Sam nodded and watched as the new arrivals mingled with the other men. Hernandez seemed to be engrossed in conversation with the sentries guarding the wagons, his manner rather casual for an officer speaking to subordinates. Consuela was standing near enough to hear what was being said and Sam went to stand by her.

'Lieutenant Hernandez seems very friendly,' he remarked.

'Yes. He's just been asking those sentries about what's in the wagons. He seemed very interested to hear about the weapons but then I suppose a soldier would be, wouldn't he?'

'I guess so,' conceded Sam reluctantly. However, there was something disturbingly familiar about Hernandez although he could not recall having seen him before. Dismissing the thought from his mind, he went off to get some supper.

Paolo felt uncomfortable in his uniform and was not used to carrying a rifle all the time. He cheered up, though, when Chico told him about the weapons.

'The Apaches would pay good money for those rifles,' he told his brother.

'Maybe, but Maximilian would pay more and Tacambaro's not far from his headquarters in Mexico City. We must bide our time until we get nearer our destination.'

'Then we can avenge our brother's death, ditch

these uniforms and sell the weapons,' added Paolo.

Chico nodded. 'Just control that temper of yours until then,' he warned him.

Night fell and passed uneventfully until they rose at dawn and prepared for another day's ride. Paolo had kept himself out of trouble and was busy grooming his horse when he noticed the woman. She was a few years older than him but somehow that only added to her appeal. His experience with women, however, had so far been limited to those whose favours one had to buy. This one was clearly different but he was confident that his manliness and charm would win the day.

Consuela was startled to find the young soldier blocking her path but he moved sideways with her as she tried to get past.

'There's no need to be in such a hurry, *señorita*. Why don't you tell me your name?'

Consuela did not reply but tried to brush past him, only to find that the young man had seized her arm.

'Come on, can't you just be a little friendly? I only want to talk to you.'

'Please, just let me past,' she replied coldly.

Some of his companions were watching and Paolo's cheeks flushed with embarrassment when one of them called out, 'Send her over here. She needs a man to satisfy her, not a boy like you.'

'Just be nice for a minute, will you? Don't shame me in front of my friends.'

Consuela pulled away abruptly. 'If there is shame

you bring it on yourself. A proper man does not treat a woman this way. Go home to your mother!'

This last comment was heard by Paolo's companions who jeered at him in response and he quickly grew angry. Just who did this haughty bitch think she was? He seized both her arms and drew her body roughly against his own.

'I'll show you what a proper man does,' he told her as he pressed his lips down hard against hers. She tried in vain to push him away while just at that moment Sam approached. Seeing what had occurred, he grabbed Paolo and spun him round before sending him sprawling with a punch to the jaw.

The Mexican quickly recovered and sprang to his feet, drawing a knife as he did so. Sam stepped aside as the younger man lunged and Paolo then spun around to rush at him again. This time Sam grabbed his arm and the two of them stood grappling for a few moments. His adversary was strong, however, and the blade inched closer to his throat as Sam tried to fight him off. Eventually, he brought his knee up sharply into Paolo's stomach and twisted his opponent's arm so that the knife dropped to the floor. Then Sam brought his fist up hard under the Mexican's chin. Paolo fell back on to the ground but this time he lay there dazed and did not get up again.

At that moment, Hernandez approached them. 'What's going on here?' he demanded, glancing down at Paolo's inert form.

'It seems your men are badly in need of discipline, Lieutenant. This one tried to molest Miss Martinez.'

Hernandez frowned hard and told one of his men to fetch some water. When the bucket was brought to him he poured it over Paolo and the young man stumbled to his feet. The officer stood over him berating him in Spanish and struck him several times. He then sent him back to join his companions before turning to Consuela.

'Please accept my apologies, *señorita*. I can assure you that the man who has offended you will be punished.' Then he bowed stiffly and made a great show of giving orders to his men, kicking several of them as he urged them to smarten themselves up.

'It's all very well doing that now but he's been letting them behave like bandits ever since they got here,' grumbled Consuela.

Sam pondered her words for that was precisely what troubled him about Hernandez and his men. They really were more like bandits than soldiers.

CHAPTER TEN

Fontaine looked through his telescope and observed the column moving ahead. He had watched the additional rebel soldiers arrive yesterday but this made no difference to his plans. The fracas that morning showed that the new arrivals had little in the way of discipline or self control but unless a major fight broke out between the two sides, he would keep following and make his move in Tacambaro.

'I told you to keep your temper. Do you want to ruin everything?' Chico hissed at his brother as they saddled their horses.

'I was trying to have a little fun,' protested Paolo. 'It was the *gringo* who caused all the trouble.'

'Well just stay away from the woman. Once we get our hands on those weapons, you'll have enough money to buy all the fun you want.'

'I'll get even with that *gringo*, though.'

'You'd best leave him to me. I'd say he's killed tougher men than you.'

Paolo opened his mouth to protest but Chico raised a hand to silence him. 'That's enough. Now come on, let's get going.'

Sam and Boyd observed the furtively whispered conversation with unease. Hernandez and the young soldier stood closely together, looking more like co-conspirators than an officer and his subordinate.

'Those two look shifty, don't they, sir?'

'That's just what I was thinking, Sergeant.'

'Still, as long as they don't interfere with us I guess it ain't none of our business.'

'It'd be best to keep an eye on them, just the same,' Sam told him.

Boyd saluted smartly and clambered on to his horse. The captain was right, come to think of it. These new arrivals were a suspicious lot and probably light fingered. He resolved to ride near the wagons for the rest of the journey, just to make sure nothing went missing from their precious cargo. After all, the cannons and explosives had already been lost so he could at least try to ensure that the rifles and ammunition remained intact.

They continued on their way, unaware that Fontaine was tracking them. Sam told Alvarez about the incident which had occurred that morning and of the conversation he had witnessed between the two Mexicans.

'I'll send a few of my men further back to keep those wagons surrounded. I don't trust that Hernandez or his rabble,' said the colonel in reply.

140

Chico noticed that more soldiers were guarding the wagons and that his own men were being watched carefully. He silently cursed his impetuous younger brother for a fool but all he could do was bide his time. An attack at night would probably be the best option, he decided, for when the enemy's suspicions were already aroused, it was more important to use the element of surprise. Then his patience would be rewarded with both the taste of revenge and the enjoyment of riches.

Chico's men, however, were getting restless. They were used to having a strong leader and obeying his orders but they were not used to uniforms and army discipline. They liked to fight, get drunk and chase women but these pastimes were denied to soldiers on duty.

'How long must we wait?' grumbled Luis Valdez, a fat, swarthy individual who was dressed in a corporal's uniform. 'I'm sick of playing at cavalry while that one-eyed *gringo* bastard watches us every step of the way.'

'Be patient, Chico knows what he is doing,' replied Hugo Montoya, his thinner companion.

'Manuel would never have got us into this mess, Hugo. We'd be better off out of it instead of trudging through these mountains dressed up like idiots.'

'Manuel got a lot of men killed,' Hugo reminded him. 'We all swore to follow Chico and no-one's going to desert him now, especially when there's a chance to get rich. Besides, if you were so fond of Manuel, shouldn't you be ready to avenge his death?'

141

Luis shrugged his round shoulders. 'Manuel's in the ground and nothing I do will help him now. These Juaristas suspect us already so I say we should get away from them as soon as it's dark.'

'Many men are afraid, Luis, but it takes a coward to run out on his friends.'

The fat bandit rounded angrily on his companion and struck him with his fist. Hugo tumbled to the ground while the rest of the column turned to witness the commotion. Hernandez rode up to Luis and demanded to know what was going on but Alvarez had now approached from the head of the column and interrupted their exchange.

'Lieutenant Hernandez, these men of yours are a disgrace! They do not wear their uniforms with pride or treat officers with respect. Worse than that, they force themselves on defenceless women and fight among themselves like common thieves!'

'Sir, I—'

'Do not interrupt me, Hernandez! When we reach Tacambaro, all these men will be confined to barracks until they learn proper discipline. As for you, I shall see to it that your new commanding officer learns of your deficiencies. Do I make myself clear?'

'Yes, sir,' replied Chico morosely as he saluted, all the while wishing he could thrust his knife into the older man's guts.

Alvarez then turned his attention to Luis Valdez. 'As for you, remove those stripes from your sleeve. You're clearly unfit for the rank of corporal.'

To his amazement, the fat man smirked in response. 'It's OK, Colonel. I quit anyway.' Then he turned his horse and rode away from the column.

'Come back here at once!' bawled Alvarez after him. 'I warn you, I'll shoot!'

Luis rode on as Alvarez drew his pistol and carefully took aim. Chico tried to remonstrate with him, promising to give chase and bring the deserter back but the colonel ignored him and fired twice. Luis tumbled from his horse and lay still.

'That is how you maintain discipline, Lieutenant. The penalty for desertion is death – you know that. We do not persuade our men or plead with them. We give them orders and they obey. Is that understood?'

Chico swallowed hard. 'Yes, sir. Perfectly understood.'

Alvarez returned to the head of the column and they began moving again. Consuela translated what had been said although Sam and Boyd guessed much of it from what they had seen. The lieutenant appeared lost in thought as he rode alongside his men, some of who whispered among themselves about what had happened.

'Can I suggest that we make our move tonight?' Hugo whispered to Chico once they were unobserved. 'The men were already getting restless before Luis was killed and now they are eager to see what you are going to do about it.'

'Yes, it will have to be tonight,' agreed Chico.

*

Fontaine came across the bandit's corpse a couple of hours later, by which time a gang of buzzards were busily tearing flesh from the dead man's bones. The two bullet holes in his back were still clearly visible, however, and Fontaine guessed that he was probably a deserter. He chuckled to himself as he continued his journey. At least there was one less enemy to worry about.

The atmosphere remained tense when they made camp that night and Alvarez posted additional sentries on duty. The afternoon's events had made him even more suspicious of Hernandez and his men so he was taking no chances. For his part, Chico passed the word among his followers of what they were to do and they made themselves ready. He and Hugo were to take care of the sentries posted near the wagons while Miguel Santos, an experienced fighter, would be assisted by Paolo to silence those at the other side of the camp.

They waited until midnight. A full moon provided enough light to guide them as they approached their targets, while the cover of darkness prevented them from being seen. Chico boldly walked up to one of the men on duty, holding out a cigarette.

'I can't sleep. Do you have a match?' he asked.

The soldier fumbled inside his tunic, looking down as he did so. He barely made a sound as the machete sliced across his throat and Chico caught his body as it crumpled to the ground, then dragged it behind one of the wagons. He was joined by Hugo who had expertly slid a knife between the ribs of another sentry and was also hiding the corpse. Chico held up two fingers to indicate the number of guards remaining and pointed to a shadowy finger about ten feet away from them. Hugo nodded and padded silently up behind his quarry. A gloved hand clamped over the mouth and a twist of the knife followed, leaving a third man dead. The fourth sentry sensed something behind him and half turned as Chico reached him. The man's cry of alarm was choked off by a stab to the heart but the bandit froze in alarm nonetheless. Had anyone heard?

Relief flooded through Chico as the silence continued. He rejoined Hugo and they went to find their two companions. Miguel and Paolo had done their work efficiently and now all eight sentries had been disposed of. The rest of the gang were all awake and would be ready to go among the sleeping rebels with their machetes as soon as the signal was given. Chico estimated that they might manage to kill half of them before the others awoke and then there would be some shooting. However, the remainder would be surprised and outnumbered so he was confident of victory.

'Are you going to give the signal now?' whispered Paolo.

'No, we must kill Alvarez and the two *gringos* first. You wait here.'

Hugo made his way to the tent in which Alvarez

slept. Pulling aside the flap, he crept inside and approached the figure huddled under the blankets on the camp bed. He raised the knife and plunged it into something soft and yielding but it was certainly not a body. Pulling the covers aside, he gasped in surprise at the pile of pillows.

'Surely you didn't think I was just going to lie there and wait, did you?'

Hugo turned towards the voice and Alvarez stepped forward from the shadows, holding a pistol. He fired just once and the bullet struck Hugo straight between the eyes, the look of astonishment remaining on his features as he fell back, dead.

In the next tent, Chico and Miguel froze at the sound of the shot. Sam's eyes opened and he fired the pistol he held concealed under his bedclothes. Chico fell back, clutching his chest and Miguel turned to flee. He was just emerging from the tent when Boyd shot him in the back. The last thing the bandit heard was the trumpet being blown in alarm. The whole camp was awake now and cutthroats who had expected to slaughter sleeping men found themselves confronted by soldiers who were armed and ready to fight.

The bandits were taken by surprise, outnumbered and outgunned by a more disciplined enemy. Gunfire echoed into the night sky as the Juaristas rose up against their leaderless assailants. Paolo could not believe what was happening but realized that his brother was dead when he saw the two *gringos* emerge from their tent and start firing at his companions. Tugging a pistol from his belt, he ran towards them with a cry of rage, only to be cut down by gunfire before he got near enough to shoot.

Bandits continued falling to the ground until only a handful remained alive. They retreated in disarray and only two managed to reach their horses and ride out of camp. It was too dark to bother giving chase but there seemed little point in doing so when the survivors no longer posed any threat to Alvarez and his men. The brief battle was over and, after burying the dead sentries, they all settled down to get what sleep they could.

Enrique Diaz and his brother Alberto rode as swiftly as they could, not stopping until they were several miles away. Both men were very lucky to have survived but were gifted with an acute sense of self-preservation, matched only by their greed and ruthlessness. At length, they slowed their horses to a halt and spotted a camp-fire just ahead of them.

'It looks like this *gringo* is alone,' whispered Enrique, the elder of the two.

'Do you think he's worth robbing?' asked Alberto.

'Well, he's got a good horse.'

The two men crept forward and were greeted by a loud click as Fontaine sat up and cocked the rifle he pulled out from beneath his blanket. 'That's far enough,' he told them in Spanish. The brothers stopped and raised their hands abruptly.

'Let me guess. You were with that outfit Alvarez is

147

leading, weren't you?'

Enrique narrowed his eyes suspiciously. 'What's that to you?'

'I want what's in those wagons and I've a score to settle with those two Americans who were with you.'

Alberto smiled as he and his brother put their hands down. 'It looks like we both want the same thing. Do you have a plan?'

'Come and have some coffee. I'll tell you all about it.'

The two Mexicans listened intently as Fontaine outlined what he intended to do, now that he had enlisted some help.

'It sounds very risky, *señor*. Are you sure it will work?' Enrique asked.

Fontaine shrugged; 'Nothing's certain, *amigo*, but I think it's worth a try. Are you both in?'

The brothers exchanged glances. 'We're in,' they replied in unison.

Alvarez allowed the men to sleep late the next morning and the sun was blazing overhead as they left camp, heading into the lower ranges of the Sierra Madre del Sur. They plodded through dry forests overlooking a valley split by the meandering Rio Balsas and finally entered the state of Michoacan. They were approaching the last leg of their journey and now Tacambaro itself was tantalizingly close.

'Just a few more days and it will all be over,' observed Consuela.

'Yes, I'm just about done with soldiering,' said Sam with obvious relief.

'Don't you like the army?'

'I guess I've just had enough of fighting. I think I might find a quiet town someplace that needs a good sheriff.'

'I see. No more battles for you then,' she said quietly. Consuela strove to hide her disappointment. She had hoped that Sam would continue fighting alongside her for the freedom of Mexico, imagining a life together when the war was over. Now she felt foolish, for it was obvious that he wanted nothing more than to return to his own country.

'I imagine you'll be relieved when all this is over,' he suggested tentatively.

'For us Mexicans it is not so simple,' she replied tartly. 'We must keep fighting to free ourselves, but, of course, it is not your fight.'

'Have I said something wrong?' Sam asked, resenting her harsh tone.

Consuela shrugged. 'You merely spoke the truth,' she told him before riding on ahead.

'That's women for you,' remarked Boyd.

'I was thinking of asking her to come back with me. It just shows how wrong a man can be,' said Sam bitterly.

Boyd chuckled knowingly. 'The way I figure it, she was hoping you'd stay behind with her. It looks like you both made a mistake.'

'Why that's crazy,' protested Sam. 'I can't just drop

149

everything and start fighting other people's wars.'

'Pardon me, sir, but isn't that what we're doing now? Besides, is expecting her to leave Mexico behind for you any more reasonable?'

Sam thought for a moment. 'Damn it, Sergeant. Why do you have to be so right all the time?'

Boyd chuckled once more. 'I guess it comes from being a bachelor.'

They stopped for the night before reaching the pine forests of the upper ranges and another two days passed without incident. Consuela remained coolly polite towards Sam while he feigned a similar indifference towards her. Meanwhile, Alvarez kept his men disciplined and focused on the task ahead as their destination loomed nearer.

Fontaine and his new companions remained some distance behind as they continued to track the column. By his reckoning, they should reach Tacambaro the next day. He patted the two bags of gunpowder he carried with him.

'Will you have enough to do the job?' Enrique asked anxiously.

'What I've got here will blow a couple of buildings sky high. We'll have plenty of time amidst all the confusion to seize those wagons and head for Mexico City.'

'What if the Juaristas come after us?' wondered Alberto.

'You're both in uniform. If anyone tries to stop

150

you, just say you're moving the wagons to safety because of the explosion. We'll be long gone before anyone realizes what's happened and they won't want to follow us right into Maximilian's territory.'

'Very well, we'll do things your way,' conceded Enrique. 'After all, you die too if anything goes wrong.'

Fontaine said nothing. He knew that neither man would hesitate to betray him should their plan come unstuck, for they were determined to save their own necks above all else. Nevertheless, he had run out of options and this last gamble was the only chance left. By the end of tomorrow, either he or Sam Curtis would lie dead in the dust.

Night fell once more and they slept peacefully under the stars after making camp out in the open. Then, in the cool of the dawn, the column set off for Tacambaro, which Alvarez hoped to reach by noon. High above sea level, they rode through mixed forests of oak, pine and cedar, surrounded by vast expanses of volcanic rock. Consuela remained distant and Sam ignored her for much of the journey. At last they entered the town itself. Sam took in the tiled roofs on the whitewashed houses as they cantered through the cobbled streets and eventually they reached the plaza in the centre where a fountain played in the sunshine.

Upon closer inspection, however, Tacambaro bore the scars of a brutal conflict. There were walls pockmarked with bullets and the church remained a burnt-out ruin. The Belgian troops stationed in the town had retreated there and the republican forces had set fire to it before their commander ordered the execution of the survivors. Rebel soldiers wandered the streets and Alvarez accosted one of them.

'We have brought weapons to help you to hold this town. Take us to your headquarters.'

The man led them to a large colonial building with a courtyard surrounded by a wall. There were some outbuildings used to store supplies; officers were quartered in the main house and their men bivouacked in tents outside. An officer approached them, saluted Alvarez smartly and introduced himself as Captain Alfredo Camorra. He and the colonel exchanged a brief conversation in Spanish before Camorra was shown the contents of the wagons. Sam and Boyd were then beckoned forward.

'We are indebted to you both for bringing us these much needed weapons. Not only will they help us to hold our position here but there should be enough rifles to supply our comrades in the mountains and forests that surround us,' Camorra told them.

'Captain Camorra was telling me that even if Tacambaro falls, a tactical retreat with these weapons means all will not be lost,' explained Alvarez. 'If the Juaristas are kept supplied with arms, eventually they will reach Mexico City and Maximilian's reign will be over.'

'I'm glad it's all been worth it,' Sam told him.

'I can assure you that all your efforts have not been in vain. Now, it is past noon so perhaps you gentlemen and this young lady would care to join me for lunch. My sergeant will see that your men are billeted and fed out here with our troops.'

Thanking Camorra for the invitation, Sam and Boyd dismounted as their host lifted Consuela down from her horse. He treated her with great gallantry, kissing her hand and linking her arm through his as he led his guests over to the house. Sam felt a surge of irritation as she responded coquettishly, laughing at some joke he made as she leant towards him. Consuela glanced briefly behind her and he caught a hint of a smile when she noticed his expression before she turned away again.

'I think she's trying to make you jealous,' remarked Boyd as they followed behind.

Sam snorted in response but said nothing, telling himself that it was of no consequence to him how Consuela chose to conduct herself. She could damn well marry Camorra tomorrow for all he cared.

Lunch was served in a long dining room where they sat in high-backed chairs around an oak table. Soup was followed by a spicy beef dish, served with goblets of wine. Camorra focused his attention on Consuela throughout the meal while she appeared to hang on his every word. Sam pecked at his food, remaining silent and morose while Boyd tucked in heartily. Alvarez was enjoying this unexpected

153

opportunity to experience the comfortable life he had known before the war and lit one of the cigars he now only indulged in rarely.

'At least I'll be going home soon,' thought Sam. After all, what else was there to keep him here in Mexico?

CHAPTER ELEVEN

Fontaine rode into Tacambaro with the Diaz brothers while Sam and the others were finishing their leisurely lunch. It did not take them long to locate the grand house and no-one challenged them as they entered the courtyard, where soldiers busied themselves with their tasks. Fontaine spotted a man wheeling a barrel into one of the outbuildings and signalled his companions to wait while he followed him on foot.

The soldier wheeled the barrel into place alongside the other stores and stopped to mop his face with a handkerchief. Fontaine clubbed him over the head with his gunbarrel and then dragged him behind some sacks of grain, where he quickly relieved the hapless soldier of his uniform. Returning to his horse, he picked up the two bags of gunpowder and slung them both over his shoulder as if he was merely carrying more stores to the storeroom.

'The *gringos* are having lunch over in the main house,' whispered Enrique who had fallen into conversation with one of Camorra's men. 'The wagons are at the other end of the yard waiting to be unloaded.'

'Excellent. It's all working out. We'll light the fuse first and the explosion will cover the sound when we shoot Curtis and the others. Then we'll head for the wagons and get out during the confusion.'

'Why not leave the *gringos*? Killing them could delay us,' protested Alberto.

'Curtis is like me. He's relentless and he'll be on our tail if we don't fix him now.'

Enrique nodded. 'Señor Fontaine is right. Let's go; we're wasting time.'

The three men headed for the outbuilding and found a corner behind some shelves. Working quickly, Fontaine hid the sacks among some bags of flour and laid a long, winding fuse behind some barrels before finally lighting it.

'If anyone comes in, they won't spot that,' announced Fontaine, confidently. 'Now, come on, we've got less than five minutes before the whole thing blows.'

Sam sat back from the table. 'I guess I'd better go see to the unloading of those weapons.'

'Relax, Captain Curtis, there is plenty of time,' said Camorra as he poured him another glass of wine.

'All the same, I think I'll just stretch my legs.' He rose to his feet and headed towards the door. As he opened it, however, he heard footsteps along the corridor which led to the dining room. He peered out and saw three men advancing towards the room, one of whom was none other than Henry Lucius Fontaine.

Sam shut the door quickly and, noticing that there was a key in the lock, turned it quickly. Then he drew his revolver and turned towards the others.

'It's Fontaine!' he hissed and Boyd immediately drew his weapon.

'That's impossible,' said Alvarez.

'Who's Fontaine?' asked Camorra.

'He's an extremely dangerous man,' Sam told him as he hurried back towards the table, gesturing for them all to get up. The footsteps had stopped outside the door as Sam turned the huge table over, sending dishes and cutlery clattering to the floor. They all crouched behind it, pistols cocked as the door handle was turned slowly.

There was a brief silence as Fontaine and his companions realized something was up and considered their next move. The door was kicked open with a splintering crash but their assailants had flattened themselves against the walls of the corridor and no shots were fired. Sam peered over the top of the table. He could see no one.

'What are they waiting for?' asked Camorra.

A moment later, the deafening sound of an explosion masked the sounds of gunfire as a volley of shots ripped into the table in front of them. Sam rolled out along the floor and fired quickly at a figure darting behind the door frame. Alberto Diaz was hit in the leg and stumbled forwards so that the side of his body was clearly visible. Sam squeezed his trigger twice more and the bandit slumped to the ground with a choked cry as the bullets thudded into his ribs.

Sam ducked back behind the table as Boyd poked his gun around the other side. At that moment, Enrique leaned around the edge of the door to fire at them and Boyd's shot caught him with a flesh wound on the side of the head. He fell back and Alvarez fired over the top of the table, hitting him squarely in the throat. As the Mexican crumpled to the ground, Sam heard the sound of running and looked over the table to see Fontaine making his escape down the corridor. He fired again but missed and cursed loudly as he ran for the door, Boyd at his heels.

'Come on, he'll head for one of the wagons,' Sam told the sergeant as they gave chase. Outside, all was confusion as men milled around fetching buckets to put out the fire caused by the explosion. The store-room had been completely destroyed and the flames were now spreading to the adjacent buildings. As the smoke cleared, Sam saw a man running towards the far end of the courtyard.

'There he is!' The two men sprinted after him as Fontaine, realizing that he was being pursued, turned and fired at them. Boyd stumbled forward with a cry as the bullet thudded into his shoulder and Sam turned to him in alarm.

'I'll be fine. You just go get him, sir,' gasped the sergeant and, after a brief hesitation, Sam ran on. As he approached the wagons, however, Fontaine was nowhere to be seen. Then a shot whizzed past his ear and he realized that the wily ex-confederate had hidden behind one of them, then waited for him to catch up. Sam dived to the ground and spotted a pair of boots. He fired at them between the wheels and was rewarded with a cry of pain. He moved around the side of the wagon to get a better shot but his quarry had vanished once again. Then he looked down, spotted a trail of blood on the ground and followed it, tentatively.

Moving swiftly but keeping alert, Sam reached the ruins of the church and stepped into the roofless interior. The building was no more than a shell, littered with burnt fragments. A blackened statue of the Virgin Mary stood on a plinth by the remains of an altar. To his left a crumbling flight of steps led to the remains of the bell tower. At that moment, Sam felt something drip on to his shoulder but did not stop to glance at the trickle of blood running down his shirt. Instead he dived to the ground, rolled and fired repeatedly up at the wounded man above him.

The bullets thudded into Fontaine's chest and he fell from the bell tower to land in a crumpled heap on what remained of the altar steps, his grey eyes staring sightlessly at the sky above the ruined church.

Sam sat down on the floor and stared at what was left of his adversary. There was no satisfaction in killing the man, just an immense feeling of relief that it was all finally over.

He turned as Consuela ran into the church. She gasped when she saw Fontaine's body and then dropped down beside him.

'Darling, are you hurt?'

He shook his head numbly and then her arms were around his neck as she kissed him over and over again. Consuela spoke rapidly in Spanish, of which he understood just enough to know that she wished only for them never to be parted.

'Do you think Colonel Alvarez needs a good staff officer?' he asked her.

'Do you really mean it? You really want to stay?'

'I'll have to go back, just to get discharged properly,' he told her. 'So here's the deal. We get married back in Texas and then it will be *viva Mexico*. What do you say?'

'Oh yes, *viva Mexico*,' she said, kissing him again.

Boyd clutched his wounded shoulder as he watched them from the ruined doorway; 'Yeah, maybe I should get some of that "*viva Mexico*" too,' he added.